PROTECTOR

A TANNER NOVEL - BOOK 30

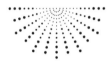

REMINGTON KANE

YEAR ZERO
PUBLISHING LLC

INTRODUCTION

PROTECTOR – A TANNER NOVEL – BOOK 30

Tanner seeks to keep his father-in-law alive after Warren Blake is targeted for death by a powerful client whose case he lost.

ACKNOWLEDGMENTS

I write for you.

—Remington Kane

BEST LAID PLANS

CONNECTICUT

Z<small>ANDER</small> H<small>ALL</small> <small>LEFT HIS VEHICLE AND STEPPED OUT</small> into a rainy evening. He moved into the shadows of the trees as he began the trek toward the remote bungalow where his wife was meeting her lover.

The small structure was off in the woods and had been constructed on land that had once held a hunting cabin. It was bordered on its west side by a state park.

When the owner of the cabin died and left it to his daughter, she had converted it into a small home. Nearby was a minuscule lake that had been dug so that she could claim it sat by the water and charge more for rent. The lake wasn't much to look at, contained no fish, and was a draw for mosquitoes. Still, it was a body of water and allowed its owner to profit by having a house with a waterfront view. The current tenant was Douglas Stanton, a personal trainer.

Zander Hall's wife, Mariana, was thirty years younger than Hall, blonde, and beautiful. Her lover, Stanton, was even younger, and as handsome as they came. Hall was not handsome, nor young. He planned to kill Doug Stanton and frame his wife for the murder.

While he was angry about the affair, Hall had another motive for wanting his wife to suffer. Mariana had met with a divorce attorney three days earlier for a consultation. She had no idea that her husband or anyone else was aware of that fact. Hall knew more than Mariana could imagine. He'd bugged her phone and often had her followed.

Zander Hall was not the type of man who would sit by and see his wealth decimated by a divorce. He was also not someone who would put up with a cheating spouse.

In his early years, Hall had been a biker who rode with a notorious motorcycle gang involved in drugs and contract murder. By his mid-twenties, Hall became interested in business; legitimate business, that is. He had a nest egg hidden away, money he had earned for transporting drugs and committing murders. He used it to open up a bar.

The bar was successful, and Hall opened a second one, then a third; over time, he grew his business into a chain of upscale taverns. They were a handy way to launder the illegal funds generated by his friends in the motorcycle gang, for a healthy percentage of course.

Hall went on to find success in the restaurant business as well. In his forties he borrowed against his restaurants, bought a second home in Nevada, and acquired a minority share in a new casino/hotel.

That enabled him to triple his wealth in a few short years, but Hall had grown impatient and wanted more. That was when he began using tactics he had learned in his former life as a biker. Within a year he'd gained control of the casino through manipulation, threats, and the timely elimination of rivals.

He had been able to accomplish his rise to the top with the help of an old friend, Cyrus Daly. While Zander Hall was a hulking figure of a man with a full graying beard and wary dark eyes, Daly was thin-framed, short, and had the cherry cheeks and bright blue eyes of a choir boy. Daly's innocuous looks were deceptive. He was far from innocent, a sadist, and like Hall, utterly without morals.

Zander Hall considered Cyrus Daly his go-to

guy. When he told Cyrus about his plan to kill his wife's lover, Cyrus asked him why he didn't let him handle it.

"I want to be the one to kill him. The asshole is screwing my wife. I want to let him know that he fucked with the wrong man."

"It's risky, Zander. If something goes wrong you've got a lot to lose."

"Nothing will go wrong," Hall told him.

BEFORE EMERGING FROM THE TREES, HALL PULLED on a black ski mask. It would have fooled no one who knew him. Zander Hall was a large man with huge hands and a distinctive lurching way of walking. The lurch was a result of a motorcycle crash that had caused him to need a hip replacement.

The bungalow consisted of a bedroom that sat off the living room. A section of the living room was partitioned off by a counter, with a kitchen area. Adjacent to the bedroom was the bathroom.

Mariana and her lover were in bed when Hall used a key to unlock the front door. Cyrus had acquired the spare key when he'd broken in to hide listening devices seven days earlier. It had been a week in which Zander Hall's hatred and rage had grown as he listened to the recordings of his wife and Stanton.

He could hear them in person as he shut the door behind him. They were making love.

Hall slid a knife out of its sheath and stepped lightly toward the bedroom. His eyes were filled with rage and his heart was primed for murder.

AT FIRST, MARIANA THOUGHT THE STRANGE CRY Doug Stanton made had been due to ecstasy; it wasn't pleasure that had birthed the sound, but agony.

She had been lying on her back with her thighs spread and her eyes shut. When she opened her eyes, she could make out the figure of the masked man standing hunched over the bed. The room was dark except for the light given off by a pair of red scented candles.

As the masked man raised his arm again, Mariana saw the blade glint in the candles' glow; she also saw the blood dripping from the weapon's tip.

Her lover, Stanton, rolled off her and onto the floor as he attempted to get away from his attacker. As he did so, Mariana saw that the man with the knife held something else in his other hand. It was one of Doug Stanton's tennis trophies. Before

5

becoming a personal trainer, Stanton had been a great amateur tennis player. No sooner had she identified the object when it came toward her at great speed. Mariana felt the impact for but an instant before she lost consciousness.

HALL SMASHED ONE OF STANTON'S TROPHIES AGAINST Mariana's forehead and watched her eyes roll back before her lids closed. When the police arrived, they would find the trophy gripped in Stanton's dead hand and come to the conclusion that he had managed to bean Mariana before dying of his wounds. For that to happen, Hall had to inflict more damage on the younger man.

Hall was fifty-nine and a lifelong smoker and drinker who never exercised. Had he not seriously wounded Stanton, despite his superior size, he would have lost in a fight against his wife's fit lover, knife or not.

Doug Stanton was twenty-four and in great physical condition, or he had been before Hall had plunged a blade into his back.

After rolling from the bed, Stanton ripped open his nightstand and removed a gun. As Hall came toward him with the knife again, Stanton thumbed off the weapon's safety and pulled the trigger.

When the gun failed to fire, Hall laughed at the look on Stanton's face. He'd already known about the gun thanks to Cyrus Daly. Cyrus had worked on the gun's firing pin so that it would fail to strike the bullets.

As Stanton stood there pulling on the trigger uselessly, Hall sank the blade into his ripped and finely muscled chest. The pain of the injury was excruciating. Stanton dropped the gun and collapsed to his knees.

Hall leaned down, pulled up the mask, and let Stanton see his face. He was pleased when he saw recognition flash in the dying man's eyes.

"That's right, asshole. I'm her husband. What? You thought you could just fuck my woman and not have to pay? The bitch wasn't worth it, was she?"

Stanton opened his mouth to plead for mercy but all that came out was blood. It was a result of Hall's blade piercing a lung. A minute later it was all over for Doug Stanton, as Hall delivered five more wounds. Hall was sweating and breathing heavily after the murder, as if he'd been running. It had been a long time since he'd killed a man himself and he'd forgotten how taxing an activity it was, particularly when a knife was used.

He looked at the bed where his wife lay naked. A lump was already forming on her forehead from the blow he'd delivered to her. He figured she would be out for hours. All that remained was to set the scene so that the cops would jump to the proper conclusion.

Mariana wasn't the only woman Doug Stanton had been sleeping with. The personal trainer had been very personal with his boss at the fitness center. That woman was a divorced mother of two. Hall would plant evidence at the scene that made it appear that Mariana had learned about Stanton's other lover and grew mad with jealousy, so mad that she decided to stab him to death.

Hall again had to thank his go-to guy Cyrus for obtaining a note that Stanton's boss had penned to him after one of their trysts at a motel where they always booked the same room. The hastily scribbled note praised the young stud for his sexual prowess and was signed with a lipstick kiss of red gloss. Stanton had read the note, smiled, and tossed it in the trash can. Cyrus had claimed it after breaking in to retrieve the listening device he'd hidden in the room.

Hall had that recording on a small tape player. It was his wife's cassette recorder. He had placed it on the coffee table in the living room before entering the bedroom. When the police heard what was on it, they would jump to the conclusion that it had been Mariana who had planted the listening device in the hotel room.

Mariana would be found with the knife, the murder weapon, the note, and a recording of her lover having sex with another woman, complete with intimate pillow talk. Hall figured she'd be lucky if they only gave her ten years. One thing she wouldn't be getting is help from her husband, nor the fat divorce settlement she was hoping to drain out of him.

After pressing the trophy into Stanton's hand and making sure his prints were on it, Hall bent over and lifted Mariana from the bed. She was a small woman and barely weighed a hundred pounds. Once he had her out of the bed, Hall lowered Mariana onto her bare feet, so that they would make contact with the blood seeping from Stanton's body. As he carried her into the bathroom, he made certain to let her feet hit the floor to leave behind crimson footprints.

After using the tip of the knife blade to flick on the light switch in the bathroom, Hall laid Mariana out in the tub and returned to the bedroom. Blood was everywhere. As was the blood evidence.

Hall stripped the sheets off the bed, then used them to mop up the blood covering the floor. He wanted to make it look like Mariana had attempted to clean up before stumbling into the bathroom. Cyrus had warned him that he'd never be able to make the scene fit the story perfectly, but that he had to at least confuse things. Hall had taken his advice.

Knowing he couldn't help but leave shoe prints behind, he had worn a pair of shoes that had the front part removed so that his stocking feet stuck out. Hall wore a size 13EEE shoe. The ones he had crammed his feet into were size 10s. The victim, Stanton, wore a standard size 10 shoe. And yeah, he was barefoot, but again, it would confuse things.

Hall used a corner of a sheet to smear the bloody prints on the bathroom tile while making certain to leave two of Mariana's footprints intact. After standing in the doorway of the bathroom and looking at the carnage in the bedroom, Hall figured he was ready to leave. Once he was outside and back at the car, he would strip naked, clean himself with wet towels he'd brought with him, and change into fresh clothes. On his way home he would use a burner phone to text Cyrus and tell him to make an anonymous call to the police. Cyrus could tell them that he'd been out for a walk and heard an argument and a man's screams.

Before leaving, Hall turned on the water in the shower. He had to make it look as if Mariana had attempted to clean herself after committing murder. If she were discovered the way she was, a blood spatter analyst would know she hadn't been the one wielding the knife that killed Stanton, as the spray patterns would be off. If she were found clean, it would be assumed she washed to be free of blood.

While there was a risk that the warm spray might rouse her, Hall didn't think so. If he had hit her any harder with the trophy she might have died.

He finished cleaning her and shut off the spray. Mariana was still out and unmoving. Hall stood in the doorway between the bathroom and the bedroom turned sideways, as he was too wide to fit in the doorway otherwise. His eyes were taking in the scene of death as he wondered if he had forgotten anything. He was certain he hadn't.

Hall had taken a step into the bedroom, ready to leave the house, when he heard the single word muttered by Mariana. That word had been his name.

"Zander?"

He turned to look back at her with the mask still on, a mask that would deceive no one, especially not a wife.

"You weren't supposed to wake up until after I left. I guess I should have hit you harder with that trophy."

Mariana stared at her husband with a look of terror lighting her face. Hall was still streaked with blood from his murder of Stanton.

"What have you done?"

"You thought I didn't know, didn't you? You thought you could just screw around behind my back?"

"You were never faithful to me."

"That's different; I'm a man."

The dull, glazed look in Mariana's eyes cleared as she revived more fully. "Oh my God, did you hurt Doug?"

"He's dead. *You* killed him."

"Dead?" Mariana said as she sat up. Distress was overcoming the concussion the blow to her head had given her.

Hall sighed. "Why couldn't you have just remained unconscious a little longer? I guess I shouldn't have cleaned you with the shower hose, but the whack on the head I gave you should have kept you knocked out."

Mariana felt the bump on her forehead. At the same time, Hall moved toward her.

"I think I need to change the plan."

Hall grabbed his wife by her hair and one arm then flipped her over. Mariana struggled, but she was no match for her husband. Hall yanked her head back before slamming it on the fixtures in the tub. He wanted to make it look like she had passed out while showering and hit her head a second time. Mariana's face collided with the metal knobs with enough force to damage the fixture and send water spraying in several directions. The blow had accomplished Hall's intention. It had killed his wife.

Hall released the body and let it flop into the tub. Mariana lay on her back with blood seeping from a cut across the bridge of her nose and another at her right temple. Spray from the damaged fixture was hitting her eyes but they remained open and unblinking. More water joined it as Hall turned the shower back on.

Hall sighed. He would have preferred seeing her rot away inside a prison. Still, he couldn't risk that since she had been aware he had killed Stanton.

As he gave Mariana one last look, he smiled. "You wanted our marriage to end? Well, you just got your wish."

Hall left the bungalow, removed his gloves, changed back into his normal shoes, then took off his mask. The cool night air felt good as it caressed his sweaty face.

The sky was cloudy, but the rain had stopped while he'd been inside. As he trudged back across the grass to where he'd left the vehicle he'd arrived in, he reminded himself to change the license plates on the car when he was done with it.

The vehicle had undoubtably been picked up by a traffic camera or some homeowner's doorbell camera. It was getting so you couldn't go anywhere without being filmed. The SUV's windows were heavily tinted and, because of his size, Hall had the seat pushed back as far as it could go. A traffic camera would have only filmed his chest or stomach. If his face had been captured on video, he would appear to be a man with long hair wearing glasses, as he had worn a disguise. Of course, the rain and the beating windshield wipers were a help too.

The SUV was stolen but wouldn't be reported missing until its owner, an ER nurse, left the hospital after working a night shift. Cyrus had acquired the SUV for Hall. As an added precaution he had given Hall a set of license plates from a same model SUV to switch out for the vehicle's real ones. It wouldn't do for the nurse to discover her ride missing early and phone in a report. With different license plates, the risk was reduced.

Hall stripped off his bloody clothes and stuffed them in a large green trash bag. They would be burned in a barrel behind an abandoned building as he had planned earlier.

As he settled in the car again after dressing, he put on the wig and donned the eyeglasses. It was an eighteen-minute drive to the rear of the building where he would burn the clothes. Hall was pleased that he felt no fear despite driving around in a vehicle that contained proof he had committed two murders. He'd always prided himself on his nerve when he'd been a young man living a dangerous life. It was good to see that the years of being a businessman hadn't weakened him in spirit.

There was no light in the alley behind the unoccupied warehouse, other than the ambient glow seeping in from the illumination of other nearby buildings. Hall had brought along a flashlight to aid in his work.

When he'd thought he heard a sound, Hall turned his head in that direction. He spotted movement near the side of a dumpster. When he sent the flashlight's beam that way, he saw that the wind was whipping about the loose end of a piece of fabric that had been caught on an old rusty chain-link fence. He relaxed and went to work getting rid of evidence.

The barrel he placed the garbage bag in had been prepared earlier by having gasoline poured into it. The bloody clothing would be burnt to ashes. Hall leaned backwards when the fire started, as the sudden heat and flash of light was intense and blinding.

After wiping down the SUV, he was leaving the alley on foot and headed to a second stolen vehicle when he remembered the license plates. He needed to take off the plates and put the real ones back on. When the vehicle was found they wanted the police to think it had been taken for a joy ride by teens and then abandoned in the alley.

Hall took off the plates and tossed them away. They skittered under a dumpster. After putting on the car's real tags he gave them a thorough wipe with his sleeve, stood, and proceeded to leave the alley.

~

HALL'S MERCEDES WAS PARKED IN FRONT OF A residential building he owned and in which he kept an apartment. Mariana had been right when she said he had been unfaithful too, but Hall never stayed at motels. He'd had enough of them when he'd been a biker and lived on the road. He much preferred having a place of his own where he could meet women. There was also a high-priced brothel he frequented.

The front door of the building opened and out stepped Cyrus Daly. He looked at Hall with concern.

"You never sent a text. Did something go wrong?"

"I had to kill Mariana too."

"Zander, are you serious?"

"It couldn't be helped. The bitch woke up and knew who I was even with the mask on. I couldn't have her telling stories to the cops."

"How did you kill her? You didn't use the knife, did you?"

"Hell no. I still made it look like Stanton bashed her in the head. The cops will figure that out when their forensic geeks run tests on everything."

Cyrus tossed a thumb over his shoulder. "Your

alibi witnesses are here. I hope you're right about them."

"They'll play along. Hell, as much as I'm offering them, they wouldn't care if I killed their mothers."

"I still say we eliminate the risk once they've served their purpose."

"That's where you come in."

Cyrus grinned. "It will be a pleasure. I love arranging "accidents."

Zander Hall had grinned back at his friend. He'd been confident that his plan would work and that he would be in the clear. He'd been wrong. Eleven days later police arrested him for the murders of his wife and Douglas Stanton. Hall steadfastly proclaimed his innocence and hired a defense attorney with an impressive track record of success, one Warren Blake. Blake, who was the father-in-law of an assassin named Tanner.

2

CHECKMATE

TANNER'S REAL NAME WAS CODY PARKER. WHEN
Zander Hall had been murdering Mariana and her
lover, Cody had been at his ranch in Texas enjoying
the company of his wife, Sara, his baby son, Lucas,
and his friends. Two of those friends were Laura
Knight and her grandson, Henry.

Henry knew that Cody was Tanner and was
eager to someday train to follow in Cody's footsteps.
Cody was the seventh Tanner, and fifteen-year-old
Henry dreamed of becoming the eighth man to
claim that mantle.

Also present was Cody's good friend, Steve
Mendez, the Chief of Police of Stark, Texas. He was
also Laura's boss, as she worked as a police
dispatcher.

Sara had invited Steve for dinner since his wife, Ginny, and their kids were away for a few days visiting Ginny's sister in Dallas. Mendez had stayed in town to work on the department's budget, a task he loathed.

Laura and Henry were neighbors of the Parkers who were renting a house on their property. Although Laura was older than Sara the two got along well and Henry never missed a chance to visit with Cody.

The Knight family had only been in Stark for a short time but were settling in well. Laura was dating a neighbor named Richard Lang while Henry was seeing another member of Lang's family, a teen named Olivia.

Henry had taken to ranch life well and rode a horse nearly every day. He also practiced his shooting skills. Cody was also teaching him the basics of self-defense and Henry was studying Spanish on his own. Stark's Hispanic population was nearly thirty percent with many of them speaking Spanish. Henry had no problem finding someone he could practice his new language skills with.

Dinner had been eaten, the baby placed in his crib, and wine poured. Henry asked for some but was told he could only have soda.

"When are you and Sara traveling to New York City, Cody?" Mendez asked. Cody and Sara had told everyone that they would be visiting the New York area so that they could celebrate Lucas's first birthday with Sara's family in Connecticut.

"We'll be there in a few weeks and stay for a while. When we return, I'm going to get serious about buying cattle so we can get this ranch up and running properly."

"You should ask Colton Darby to go with you when you buy the cattle," Mendez said. "That man has forgotten more about ranching than most folks will ever know."

"My father used to say the same thing. He never bought a single head of cattle unless Mr. Darby was with him. I'll contact him when we get back."

AFTER DINNER, CODY AND MENDEZ MOVED INTO THE Parkers' home office. It was a good-sized space that had a large screen TV on one wall while the other walls were covered with books, many in other languages.

Cody and Steve settled before a chess board to continue a game they had begun the last time they'd met. Cody usually won, but Mendez was nearly his equal at the game and the outcome was always in doubt.

"They had a high school kid overdose on meth

the other day in Culver, and heroin use is on the rise in the area. One of my deputies arrested a teen who was carrying heroin. I couldn't get the kid to tell me where he'd gotten it from."

"How hard did you try?"

"Not very hard; the boy was only fourteen. I'm not roughing up a fourteen-year-old."

"If there's one kid with the drug, there are others. If you don't figure out where it's coming from it will only get worse."

"I know, but the damn mayor cut my budget again. I can't authorize more than a few hours of overtime a week with the money I have."

"You'll find the drug runners, Steve, because sooner or later it won't be a kid you arrest. Then you'll be able to play rough and get answers."

"Damn straight I'll play rough, pardner. I will not see Stark turn into a haven for drug dealers."

"I was surprised by how little this town changed in the years I was away. We both thought it was boring when we were Henry's age; we didn't realize how lucky we were to grow up in a town like this."

"Stark will be the same as long as I'm chief. That is, if that damn idiot, Jimmy Kyle, doesn't gut my department's payroll."

"Are you still considering running against him in a few years?"

"I am."

"You have my vote," Cody said, as he moved a rook on the board. That was followed by the word, "Checkmate."

3

A THREAT OR A PROMISE?

ZANDER HALL FOUGHT TO APPEAR CALM AS THE prosecutor in his murder trial laid out the State's theory of how Hall committed the murders. The prosecutor, Sherman York, was eerily correct in most instances during his opening statement. It caused Hall to wonder how they could have figured out so much.

York paused in his presentation to the jury to point at Hall. York was a thin man in his thirties with brown eyes and sandy-colored hair.

"After brutally stabbing Mr. Stanton to death, Zander Hall struck his wife with a trophy to render her unconscious. We believe his initial desire was to frame her for her lover's murder. Perhaps hatred overwhelmed him, or his wife came to and saw him, but Mr. Hall then decided to kill her, which he did by bashing her face against the fixtures in the bungalow's bathtub.

How could they know that? Hall thought, although he knew the answer. *It's those damn forensic geeks.*

It was true. Despite the precautions he'd taken, the police forensic and lab personnel had pieced together the crime and come to the conclusion that a third party had been involved. Once that deduction had been made, it was a simple step to assume that the dead woman's husband was a prime suspect.

Hall had given a statement in which he'd said that he'd been involved in a meeting at the time the murders were supposed to have occurred. Three witnesses backed him up. They were business associates Charlie Hance, Al Espinoza, and Elsa Kaplan.

Hance, Espinoza, and Kaplan supported Hall's story and gave signed statements to the authorities. Within days, all three of them met sad fates. Charlie Hance died in a hit-and-run accident as he was jogging. Al Espinoza was blown to pieces when the water heater in his home exploded. As for Elsa Kaplan, she remained missing after disappearing while on a nature hike.

They could not be called as witnesses nor could they retract their stories. If the jury believed they were telling the truth, Hall would be found not guilty. On the other hand, if the jury, like the State, found it odd that Hall's three alibi witnesses all suffered misfortune that was convenient for Hall, he might spend the rest of his life in prison.

And then there was the SUV Hall had used to travel to and from the bungalow. It had been caught on three traffic cameras, with two of them capturing the license plate numbers. Investigators concluded that it had been in the vicinity of the bungalow.

Cyrus's idea of switching out the license plates had been a good one. It had caused the police to originally suspect the owner of the license plate's vehicle, which was the same model and color as the SUV Hall had used.

As coincidence would have it, the man who owned the stolen license plates had an old arrest for assault and looked like a good suspect at first. But the license plate owner had been out of town on vacation and could prove it. It still muddied the waters and made the State's case against Hall less straightforward. Despite what they suspected about the stolen SUV, because its plates were different than the ones captured on video, there was doubt as to whether it was the vehicle the killer used.

Fortune had favored Hall as the cameras had failed to capture him well. All three of them filmed him from the chin down, showing his beard and what appeared to be long hair. While Hall had a beard, he hadn't had long hair since his biker days.

"A wig," the prosecutor said. "Mr. Hall was wearing a wig in an attempt to hide his identity. However, it's plain to see from the photos that whoever was driving the vehicle was a large man with a beard, such as Mr. Hall. It is the State's contention that his so-called alibi witnesses were paid to give false statements. Their payment would have been in the form of huge percentages of a new casino project Mr. Hall's company is involved in. Those percentages would have been worth millions in the long run.

We find it extremely convenient for Mr. Hall that those witnesses have either died or gone missing." York paused to again stare and point at the accused. "Let me assure you, all three of those instances are being investigated as well."

Hall leaned to his right and whispered to his attorney, Warren Blake. "Is he allowed to point at me like that when I'm not on the stand?"

"It's allowed," Warren said. "And you will not be taking the stand."

"Right," Hall said. "Because of the five bitches on the jury?"

"Keep your voice down. And yes, because of the *women* on the jury. The media has portrayed you as a misogynist and found plenty of instances to back up the claim. It will be difficult enough for me to win those ladies over to our side as it is. If you were to say something offensive while on the stand, we would lose them for sure."

Hall looked over at the female jurors. "They sure are ugly. I guess all the hot bitches know how to get out of jury duty."

"Zander, please be quiet," Warren said. "You never know who might be reading your lips."

"Are you serious? Lip readers?"

"The media has been known to hire them, the prosecution too."

"Shit."

The prosecutor ended his opening statement and Warren rose to address the jury. He was a distinguished-looking man with a handsome face and a full head of graying hair. He smiled at the jurors and made eye contact with each of them before speaking.

"Good morning. My name is Warren Blake and I have the privilege of defending Zander Hall against the charges being brought against him by the State. The prosecutor, Mr. York, claims my client is guilty but if you listened closely you would have noticed that he never once offered any proof of his assertion. Ladies and gentlemen, that is because no proof exists."

Warren turned to look at Hall. Instead of pointing as York had done, he sent his client a reassuring smile.

"No evidence places Zander Hall at the scene of the murders. There are no eyewitnesses or forensic evidence against him. Zero. Mr. Hall also had no idea that his wife was having an affair, nor did he know that she had met with a divorce lawyer. As far as my client knew, all was well in his marriage."

Warren held up a hand. "I do not wish to disparage the deceased; however, it appears that Mrs. Hall had been keeping secrets from her husband, not the least of which was her lover. Likewise, the second victim, Douglas Stanton, while carrying on an affair with Mrs. Hall was also engaged in a sexual relationship with his female boss. There is evidence that proves Mrs. Hall learned about that relationship and it is my contention that it drove her to commit drastic acts; acts which resulted in not only the death of Mr. Stanton, but herself as well."

Warren turned and pointed at the prosecutor. "Mr. York says that there was a third party at the scene of the murders. It may surprise you to hear me say that I agree with that statement. The fact is that the evidence of a third party is irrefutable. That said, there is not one atom of evidence that points to my client being that person. On the contrary, certain aspects of the evidence would eliminate him as being involved. Furthermore, my client can prove that he was elsewhere as the murders were occurring. Three separate individuals attested to that fact."

Warren paused again to make brief eye contact with each juror. "Your job is to determine if there is reasonable doubt. I assure you there is. My client was not at the bungalow and did not kill his wife or Douglas Stanton. Zander Hall is innocent, and by the end of the trial you will be led to that obvious conclusion. Thank you."

Warren smiled at his client as he retook his seat beside him. It felt damn good to be back in a courtroom again. As usual, he didn't know or care if his client was guilty; his only job was to give Zander Hall the best defense that he could. He thought the chances of acquittal were excellent if the case against Hall was judged solely on its merits.

Hall leaned over, shielded his lips from anyone capable of reading them, and spoke in a low growl to Blake.

"If this ends with me going to prison it will be the worst day of your life."

Warren blinked at his client in surprise. "Are you threatening me?"

"Just do whatever you have to do to make sure I go free."

Warren looked into his client's cold eyes and saw that Hall was serious. He took in a deep breath and released it slowly. He had been threatened by clients before. Of course, that had been at the start of his career when he was defending a lower class of individual. It surprised him that a businessman of Hall's stature would utter such words.

"As I stated when you hired me, Zander, you'll get the best defense I'm capable of delivering. After that, your future is in the hands of the jury."

The trial began in earnest as the prosecution called its first witness, an expert on blood spatter. And the hearing that would determine Zander Hall's fate commenced.

4

THE MAN IN CHARGE

CODY AND SARA ARRIVED IN NEW YORK CITY ON A weekday evening and went to the penthouse apartment they owned. They would only be staying there for a short time, as they had plans to visit Sara's father for a week in Connecticut.

Lucas had been walking for months. He toddled around the penthouse while occasionally pointing up at items that caught his interest.

"He was such a small thing the last time we were here. Now he's walking and talking," Sara said.

"Talking?"

"Mama and Dada count as talking."

"It's a start," Tanner agreed. Cody was Tanner when they were in New York. Sara told him that a change of attitude came over him whenever they returned to the city. It was a subtle difference, but significant. And while Cody dressed in a western style on the ranch, often donning a cowboy hat as he had done in his youth, Tanner favored leather jackets and seldom covered his head with anything other than a cap.

It was mid-March and a bit of warmth was in the air. Despite that, the forecast called for a chance of snow showers in the near future.

A paid service kept the penthouse clean and had even stocked it with food. After their week in Connecticut they would be returning to New York City. As much as they loved their home in the Texas countryside, both Sara and Cody held an affinity for New York. Being able to come and go as they pleased meant they would never grow tired of either lifestyle.

THERE HAD BEEN AN ASSASSINATION IN THE CITY overnight. The victim was a man wanted for war crimes in Bosnia. He'd lived under the radar in New York City for decades, but a bullet finally found him. When Tanner heard reporters discussing details of the killing, he became interested. The target had been killed by a rifle shot that was estimated to have been fired from over fourteen hundred yards away.

There weren't more than a handful of people in the world who could hit a target from that distance; he was one of them, as were Spenser and Romeo. He sent texts off to both of them and received responses within minutes saying that they weren't the shooter. They also agreed it was impressive.

Tanner knew of only two other men who might have been capable of such a display of marksmanship. One was dead, Maurice Scallato. The other was an Asian assassin who went by the name of Taran. Scallato had been nicknamed the Ghost. Taran was often referred to as the Shadow.

Tanner first became aware of Taran when he was in England recently. A contract he was given came close to being offered to Taran. Since that time, Tanner had a hacker named Zoe Farnsworth look into what she could find out about Taran. Zoe was the granddaughter of Tanner Five and an old friend.

There were no photos of Taran but there was a general description. He was said to be five-foot-ten, of average build, and somewhere in his thirties. What little Zoe uncovered about Taran wasn't much but echoed Tanner's own life.

Tanner had gone to war once with an organization calling itself the Conglomerate. The Conglomerate was a mixture of corporate and mob figures who were working together.

Taran had battled a similar pairing of corporate

bigwigs and a Japanese crime syndicate called Yakuza. Taran was said to have killed over a hundred of the Yakuza's members before hostilities ended. Tanner wondered if it had been Taran who had committed the impressive hit in the city the night before.

LATER THAT MORNING, SARA LOADED LUCAS INTO A car seat as she prepared to visit a friend named Alicia Kincaid who lived in Queens. As for Cody, he was going to visit Joe Pullo and have lunch with him.

"I'll meet you back here at four then we'll head off to see Daddy," Sara said.

"Right," Tanner told her. He had leaned into the back seat to give Lucas a kiss.

"If you see Laurel, tell her I'll call soon and make a date for lunch or shopping."

"I'm glad you two made peace with each other while she was staying with us a few months ago."

"I've never had a problem with Laurel; she was the one who had to forgive me for threatening her the way I did."

"You saved her life and Johnny's life when the old clinic was attacked. And risked yourself to do it. That more than evened the score, Sara."

The couple kissed, and Sara drove off. Tanner

was on foot. He always liked walking around Manhattan and fed off the energy of the city. As he moved along, a casual observer would notice nothing different about him. They would be wrong. Unlike the others around him Tanner was keenly aware of his environment.

He used the reflective surfaces of storefronts and parked cars as mirrors to observe his fellow pedestrians and swiveled his head often to keep an eye on his rear.

While stopped at the curb waiting for a traffic signal to change, Tanner witnessed a crime. A man carrying a jacket used it to shield his other hand as he unzipped and reached into the purse of a woman who was busy paying attention to the two small girls that were with her. The children were chattering excitedly about going to the zoo and the young mother was answering their questions. She had no idea that her wallet had just been stolen.

As the light changed, the woman crossed the street with her kids as the thief headed left along a side street. Tanner followed the robber and waited for an opportunity. His chance came as the man was approaching the spot where a large van was parked. The vehicle would block the view of anyone on the other side of the street or passing by in traffic, and no other pedestrians were within a block of them.

Someone in the apartment house the van was in

front of might see what happened, but by the time they reacted, Tanner would be out of sight.

The light-fingered thief tensed up as he heard Tanner rushing up on him but was too late to react. Tanner stepped on the back of the man's right knee, taking him to the ground; with his left hand he gripped the man by his shaggy hair. As the man opened his mouth to cry out, Tanner slammed his face against the pavement with enough force to render the pickpocket unconscious. It also broke his nose and chipped a tooth.

He recovered the woman's wallet, then found another one. The photo on the driver's license matched the thief. It was his own wallet. Tanner removed the money he'd found in the crook's wallet and added it to the one stolen from the woman.

IT HAD TAKEN A SEARCH OF SEVERAL BLOCKS WHILE moving along at a jog before Tanner caught up with the woman. She was stopped at the cart of a food vendor buying snacks for her kids. A look of shock came over her when she saw that her pocketbook was sitting wide open. When, after a frantic search, her hand failed to locate her wallet, she let out a moan.

"Excuse me. I think you dropped this."

The woman looked at the wallet Tanner was holding out to her. He could see the tension leave her shoulders as a sigh of relief moved past her lips.

"Oh, thank God. I thought it had been lost or stolen. I can't believe I was dumb enough to leave my bag unzipped."

"No harm done," Tanner said.

He was moving away when the woman called to him. "I should give you a reward. At least let me buy you something from the cart here."

"That's okay."

The woman had opened her wallet and was staring in with a bewildered expression. "That's weird. I don't remember having this much money."

Tanner left her to her puzzlement and blended back into the crowd.

HE WAS MEETING JOE PULLO AT A BOXING GYM THAT Joe was a part owner of, Coburn's Gym. The mob boss had taken to training as a boxer to stay in shape.

While there were a few guys working on heavy bags or sparring, the gym was quiet. Mixed martial arts had lured away many fighters. Hard-core adherents still followed the sport and there were those that would always prefer it over other violent sports. Regardless of that, being crowned heavyweight champion of the boxing world didn't have the same importance and significance it once had back when Ali, Foreman, and Tyson were kings of the sport.

Pullo emerged from the locker room with his hair still damp from the shower. He smiled when he spotted Tanner.

"I hope you weren't waiting long, buddy."

"I just got here. I was sidetracked along the way."

Joe patted his stomach. "I'm starving. These workouts give me an appetite. You just missed Finn. He rushed off to meet his girl. You should see her, Tanner, she's a beauty named Moira. And get this, she's a plumber."

"Somebody has to fix busted pipes, why not a woman?"

"Ha. Sammy said the same thing."

"How's Sammy doing these days?"

"Great. He's taken over some of Bosco's duties, along with Finn." Joe sighed. "I miss Bosco."

"Has there been any trouble from the Gants?"

"None, and it had better remain that way."

"It will if they want to stay alive. Distant relations or not, I promised I would kill them if they ever broke the truce. If it had been my decision, I would have wiped them out."

"I only made peace because we were so low on men. We lost a lot of good guys because of that damn bomb of Victor Gant's. Besides, what the hell could I do, load everyone onto a plane and head to France? Even if I did that and won the war, when I came back here, I'd find someone else sitting in my office. This is my turf. If I left it every other gang in the city would be gunning to fill the vacuum."

"Does that include Tyrese Vann and the Bloods?"

Joe smiled at Tanner as he ran a comb through his damp hair. "That guy is the only good thing to come out of that war. Tyrese does what he says and usually delivers more than promised. He runs a tight ship with the Bloods and has increased profit in the areas he's running."

"It sounds like you two have become friends."

"Yeah, he's a friend. If it weren't for the fact that he's black, I'd ask him to join the Giacconi Family."

Tanner and Joe left the gym and began walking toward the restaurant.

"Was that your work last night down in Tribeca?" Joe asked.

"The dead war criminal?"

"Yeah."

"No, that wasn't me."

"Whoever it was is a hell of a shot."

"Oh yeah," Tanner said.

They talked about their sons as they walked. Joe paused several times to speak to someone, usually an older person. They were on his turf, neighborhoods controlled and protected by the Giacconi Family, and Don Pullo was among his people.

An old lady complained about the graffiti that had been painted on the front of her apartment building. Joe told her that the matter would be looked into and that the vandalism would stop.

Tanner was wearing a long-billed baseball cap and dark sunglasses to make it difficult to identify him. Since he was with Pullo, most people probably thought he was a bodyguard and a Giacconi street soldier.

At one point, while he was glancing around, he spotted a man looking his way from a corner across the street. He was wearing a black hoodie and his features were hidden inside the folds of the hood. Straps looped over his shoulders indicated that he was wearing a backpack. Tanner lowered his sunglasses to get a better look at the man. In the instant his vision was temporarily blocked by the lowering of the sunglasses' frames, the man had disappeared. Tanner assumed he had moved around the corner. If so, his reflexes were exceptional.

THE MAN IN THE HOODIE WAS THE ASSASSIN NAMED Taran. He had been the one who had carried out the contract on the Bosnian war criminal. Before and after the hit he had been following Joe Pullo. Taran was aware that Pullo was rumored to be friends with Tanner. Taran was interested in Tanner and wanted to see the man in person. He had begun to think he'd been wasting his time until he'd spotted Pullo leaving the gym accompanied by another man. There was something about the way the man carried himself. Pullo's demeanor suggested that the two were equals, not employer and employee. The man with him was not a bodyguard or a lackey. Taran wondered if he were looking at Tanner.

He grew certain of it when Tanner spotted him. There was an aura about the man, perhaps it was something indefinable that only another assassin might perceive. Not wanting to provoke suspicion or wariness, Taran departed swiftly.

He entered a coffee shop, went to the counter, and ordered a cup of tea, along with a sandwich. As the waitress was giving his order to the cook, Taran walked into the small men's room and locked the door behind him.

After removing his backpack, Taran took off the black hoodie and folded it up. From the pack he

43

removed a blue, lightweight jacket along with an *I Love New York* baseball cap and a digital camera. He put on the jacket and the cap, then hung the camera around his neck by a strap. The hoodie was placed inside the backpack, which itself was converted to look like a duffel bag.

When Taran left the restroom moments later, he looked like many other Japanese tourists. If Tanner grew suspicious and searched for him, he should go unnoticed.

Taran sat at the counter and enjoyed his lunch as he thought about the odd message that had been passed on to him that morning. Someone was seeking to hire him to carry out a contract. However, it wasn't clear if his services would be needed, so they wanted to reserve him by offering a deposit.

He smiled. He had never been offered a down payment before. In any event, having nothing to do, he decided to stay in New York City and see what developed. He would also look into the target; in case he was given the contract. The man named as a potential victim didn't seem worthy of his skill. He was not in hiding and aware of being hunted as the Bosnian had been.

No, the man named as being a prospective target was often out in public and should have no reason to suspect that someone wanted to kill him.

That alone made the contract uninteresting to Taran. He loved a challenge. Taran took out his phone and read the message again. The man in question was a lawyer. His name was Warren Blake.

PULLO ENDED HIS CONVERSATION WITH THE OLD woman and they continued on their way.

"Walking around with you is like hanging out with a politician," Tanner told him.

"I'm the man in charge. If these people have a problem, they come to me. When I grew up on these streets, it was the same way. Everyone went to see Sam if there was trouble. He told me that if you handled the small things you saved yourself having to later deal with big problems. He was right."

"Like vandalism?"

"Today some kid sprays paint on that woman's building. Let it go and he might try to snatch her purse next. I'll have someone find the kid with the paint and have a talk with him."

"Speaking of kids, how's Adamo Conti doing?"

"That boy's all right. Maybe I'll have him handle the graffiti problem."

"What's he been doing?"

"Collections."

45

"Like dealing with late payers? The kid didn't strike me as the tough guy sort."

"He might have to make a threat or two if someone is a little light, but it's more like he's collecting the protection money. And don't sell Conti short. Look at Sammy, did you ever think he had it in him to be an enforcer?"

"No. But the kid changed after Sophia was killed."

"That's for damn sure. Thank God for his girlfriend, Julie. The girl brought him back from a dark place."

They reached the restaurant and found it crowded. It didn't matter. The Giacconis kept a table reserved in a private room at the rear of the building. As they looked over the menus, Joe asked Tanner if he had a contract in the area.

"I'm not working. This is a family vacation to celebrate Lucas's first birthday."

"They grow up fast, don't they?"

"Lucas sure is, and the boy is strong too. I'm told that great strength runs in the family. It skipped me, maybe it didn't skip Lucas."

"My boy Johnny is a lot like his mom. I think he got Laurel's brains. She's already taught him to read a little. I was terrible in school. I always wanted to be out on the streets."

"Sara said to tell Laurel that she would call her soon. It looks like our wives have become friends."

"Look at us, Tanner. We've got wives and kids. How did that happen?"

"We let our guard down and now we're paying the price."

Joe laughed. "I wouldn't change a thing."

"Neither would I," Tanner said.

A NEW WITNESS

THE MURDER TRIAL OF ZANDER HALL ENTERED ITS second week and things were looking good for the defense at the Friday break. The prosecution had a plethora of evidence that proved a third person had been present when Mariana Hall and Douglas Stanton died, but none of it explicitly pointed to Zander Hall.

Meanwhile, investigations into the deaths and disappearances of Hall's alibi witnesses were going nowhere. The hit & run death appeared to be just that and the hot water heater explosion that killed Al Espinoza was determined to be the result of a faulty installation. Espinoza, a man who made his fortune flipping houses on the cheap, had installed the water heater himself to save money.

Elsa Kaplan's disappearance continued to be a mystery. When she went missing in upstate New York, Zander Hall had been in Connecticut preparing for his wife's funeral.

Since there was no evidence to arrest him for Kaplan's disappearance, the prosecution went about trying to convict Hall in the arena of public opinion. It became widely known that Hall was once a member of a biker gang and the insinuation was that he never left the outlaw motorcyclists.

A number of women testified about Hall's disregard for the female sex and that he treated them like property. Three had been property, rented property, as in their earlier years they had hired themselves out as call girls to Hall.

Sherman York, the prosecutor, was doing his best to make Hall look like a misanthropic hater of women who couldn't bear to know that his wife was cheating on him.

Warren Blake repeatedly pointed out that there was no evidence that Hall knew of the affair. Someone who had known of an affair was the ex-husband of Doug Stanton's boss and lover. Their marriage had ended badly when that man had caught his wife in their bed with another man. That man hadn't been Stanton, he had been another employee of the health club the woman owned, and her ex-husband had gotten into a fist fight at the time.

While he didn't actually accuse the ex-husband, Warren pointed out that there was a third party involved who had a history of becoming violent when he found his wife with another man. The ex-husband also had no alibi that could be corroborated, as he'd been home alone watching TV on the night the murders took place. It was yet another way to instill reasonable doubt in the minds of the jurors.

WARREN BLAKE SAT AT HIS DESK INSIDE HIS OFFICE IN Connecticut after a day in court. He was feeling good about their chances of gaining an acquittal. That feeling began to dissipate when his investigator walked in and took a seat across from him. The investigator was an ex-cop named Gavin Knutson. He was a fit man of sixty who ran a private detective agency with his sister, Glenda. Glenda had also been a cop.

"There's a new witness in the case."

Warren had been leaned back in his chair with his feet propped up on a corner of the desk. He placed his feet on the floor and sat up straight.

"What witness?"

"A homeless vet named Victor Jenkins claims he saw Hall on the night of the murders."

"He's stating he saw Hall at the bungalow?"

"No, in an alley behind a building. It's the same alleyway where the stolen SUV was found."

"Does he offer any proof?"

"No."

"He's homeless?"

"I should have said he *was* homeless. He's living in a halfway house on Murphy Street now."

"A halfway house? So, he was a drug addict?"

"An alcoholic and a schizophrenic. He's off the booze and is on a new medication that's controlling his mental issues. He told the police he only learned about the case after getting out of a psychiatric hospital. He swears that Hall is the man he saw in the alley and that it was on the night Hall's wife was murdered."

Warren leaned back in his seat again. "You had me worried, Gavin, but this guy doesn't seem credible at all. A schizophrenic alcoholic isn't exactly an ideal eyewitness."

"I would agree except for one thing. Victor Jenkins has what they used to call a photographic memory. It means he can form eidetic images in his brain like a camera filming a scene. An ability like that might play well in front of the jury. You've got to know that some of them will look for any reason to find Hall guilty. If they think Jenkins is credible, that may wipe out reasonable doubt in their minds."

Warren knew Gavin was right. And homeless schizophrenic or not, Jenkins was a veteran who had served his country. That would also weigh in his favor.

"I want to interview him."

Gavin smiled. "I contacted him by phone. He's agreed to meet with us here tomorrow morning. I know it's the weekend, but I thought you would want to meet him as soon as possible."

"Yes, of course, and it shouldn't take long."

"I'll pick him up and bring him here since he doesn't have a car."

"Good work. How did Jenkins sound on the phone?"

"He seemed normal and certain that what he's saying is the truth. If this guy gets on the stand, he may do the case some damage."

"Yeah, but it's not the end of the world. Once I've interviewed him, I'll come up with a strategy to counter what he says. Even if the jury believes Jenkins it will still be his word against that of Hall's three alibi witnesses. I really wish I could have placed them on the stand."

"They're all dead, Warren. Does that bother you?"

Blake had been about to recite the words that he told the jury about how Hance, Espinoza, and

Kaplan's deaths and disappearance didn't negate their statements. Instead, he released a long sigh.

"Hell yeah, it bothers me. But I'm not ready to assume that Zander Hall was behind it."

"Take it from an ex-cop who's been around the block, Zander Hall is a bad dude."

"That doesn't mean he killed his wife or eliminated his alibi witnesses so they couldn't retract their stories."

"True. But if that's the case, I wouldn't want to get on his bad side."

There was a knock on the open office door. Warren looked up to see a tall and beautiful woman in her forties smiling at him. Her name was Nina Girardin. She and Warren had begun dating before the trial began and had grown close.

"Am I interrupting?" Nina asked. She had a French accent, having grown up in Marseille.

Warren smiled back at her. "Come on in; Gavin and I are about finished."

Gavin rose from his seat and offered it to Nina. "I need to be in New York City to meet with Glenda. You two have a great evening."

Gavin left and Warren rose to take Nina in his arms. After kissing, he told her he had news.

"My youngest daughter is in town with her husband and my grandson. I want you to meet them tonight."

"I look forward to it. Her name is Sara, right?"

"That's right, and you'll love her."

"What's her husband like? You don't mention him as much as you talk about your other son-in-law, the FBI agent."

"Maybe that's because I see Jake more often than I see Cody, but Cody is… he's a Texas rancher."

"A rancher? I got the impression he was an unemployed layabout."

"No, he's quite busy, and very good at what he does."

"Do you like him?"

"I do, and I never thought I would."

Nina pecked Warren on the nose with a kiss. "Why do I think there's something else about Cody Parker that you're not saying?"

"I don't know, but I think you'll like him too. Cody is intelligent and well-read. He can speak French, so you have that in common."

"How's the trial going?"

"Well, I'd say the odds are in our favor that Hall will be acquitted."

"Fantastique! Warren, we should celebrate."

"Not so fast. I learned a long time ago not to count my chickens before they've hatched."

"That's a phrase I haven't heard in years."

"Yes, but I'm ten years older than you, and a grandfather."

Nina said, "There's still some life left in you," and kissed him.

Tanner had taken precautions against being followed when he returned to the penthouse. The man in the hoodie had been odd and was possibly someone interested in him. It didn't happen often, but there had been occasions when some other assassin sought him out, looking to kill him and improve their reputation. They wound up lying dead in the street instead.

There was no sign of his hooded friend and Tanner assumed it had been nothing. Perhaps the man had been staring at Joe Pullo instead of him. He had mentioned the incident to Joe over lunch. If the man were a threat and made a move on Pullo instead, Joe would also put him down.

He and Sara arrived at Warren's home with Lucas that evening. Sara's sister, Jennifer, was there with her husband, Jake Garner, and her daughter, Emily. Emily was only two, so she and Lucas played together in the middle of the living room floor while the adults had drinks and talked.

Warren had introduced Nina to Sara and Tanner. Although Sara was cordial to Nina, Tanner could tell that his wife had misgivings about the woman. He asked her about it later in the evening when they were alone in the kitchen for a few moments.

"I don't dislike her. I... it's just that it always feels weird to me to see my father with a woman who isn't my mother. After my mother left us when I was twelve, Daddy didn't date until I went off to college."

"Why was that?"

"I think he was still hurting from Lily's betrayal, or maybe it was because of how hard I took her abandonment of us. Daddy was always there for me and Jenny, more so than most fathers. I hope Nina is the right one for him. He deserves to be happy."

WHEN HE RECEIVED A CALL TOWARD THE END OF dinner, Warren excused himself from the table and took it in private. When he returned a few minutes later, he was grinning.

"I guess you received good news," Sara said.

"That was the district attorney. He's offered us a new plea deal. That means they believe Zander Hall will be found not guilty. I think they're right."

"What was the deal?" Jake Garner asked. He was a

handsome man who turned female heads wherever he went.

"Eight years in prison with the possibility of parole in five. Hall would have to admit his guilt as well."

"Did you tell your client about the deal?" Nina asked.

"Oh yeah. He nixed it right away. Zander has been adamant that he doesn't want to spend a day in prison."

"I would care less about the time and more about admitting to something I didn't do," Jake said.

Warren frowned. "I know you think Zander is guilty, Jake. He may well be, but it's my job to defend him regardless of his guilt or innocence."

Jake held up a hand. "I understand that you're just doing your job and that you can't judge your client. It's my job to catch criminals and lock them up, and your client reeks of guilt to me."

"He may well be a murderer, but that's for a jury to decide."

Jake shrugged. "That's the system we have, and for your sake, I hope you win the case."

"I find your attitude surprising, Jake, seeing as how you're an FBI agent," Nina said. "You wish Warren luck even though you believe his client is guilty of murdering his wife?"

"Warren is family, so I support him. Besides, the

last few years have taught me to be less judgmental. Some people are guilty and no good, then there are others who, while guilty, are good people. Life's not always black and white," Jake said, while glancing across the table at Tanner. He and his brother-in-law had become friends, despite being on opposite sides of the law. Tanner sent him a slight nod as an acknowledgement.

Warren smiled at Jake. "I could use your support again on Monday morning. I'll be dropping my car off at the dealership for routine servicing and could use a ride to the office afterwards."

"No problem, Warren. I'm off until we return to the city on Wednesday. I'd be happy to give you a lift."

"Thank you," Warren said. "There's a good chance the case will go to the jury next week. The prosecution only has one expert witness left. Once I cross-examine them, that should bring things to an end."

"Do you have any other court cases pending?" Sara asked.

"No, but I hope to get one. I love being before a jury again. It's where I do my best work."

"You seem happier than I've seen you in a long time."

Warren reached to his right and took Nina's

hand. "My work pleases me, but it's Nina who makes me happy."

Nina leaned toward Warren and they kissed. Sara smiled at the couple. It was the plastic smile of a mannequin. Something about Nina Girardin didn't sit right with her.

6
GUILTY!

WARREN BLAKE'S INVESTIGATOR GAVIN KNUTSON stepped out of his car and looked up at the old building that was home to the halfway house where Victor Jenkins lived.

The entire neighborhood was rundown and everyone Gavin saw appeared as if they had fought life tooth and nail and lost badly. Even the children playing down the block looked sorrowful in their drab hand-me-down clothing.

When he spotted the young woman getting out of another vehicle behind him, he knew she wasn't a native of the area. The business suit she wore was tailored and she had the bright sheen of youth and ambition about her. She had dark hair and eyes with light brown skin. What little of her legs her skirt revealed were shapely.

As she grew closer, Gavin realized he had met her before, although he couldn't recall her name. He sighed. It was another sign that he was getting old. Twenty years earlier he never would have forgotten the name of such a lovely woman. When she reached him and extended her hand in greeting, her name returned to him and he smiled. Maybe he wasn't so old after all.

"Assistant DA Pia Gonzales, how are you?"

"I'm good, Mr. Knutson, and I can guess why you're here. You've come to talk to Mr. Jenkins."

"Actually, I'm here to pick him up and take him to Warren Blake's office for an interview."

"We thought that might happen. I'm going to ask Mr. Jenkins to refuse to speak with you. He's already given us a statement. We'll be sure to give you a copy on Monday morning."

Gavin gestured toward the building. "Let's go see what he has to say."

WARREN ARRIVED AT HIS LAW OFFICE ON SATURDAY morning to have his meeting with Victor Jenkins. Despite being a Saturday, he was dressed in a suit and tie. Once the meeting was over and he was back home, he could change into something more casual. He was looking forward to spending the rest of the day with his family, especially his grandchildren.

Knutson's call came in as Warren was setting up the office coffee maker in preparation of brewing a pot of Colombian supreme. It was good news for the defense.

"He's drunk?" Warren said.

"As a skunk," Gavin answered. "Apparently, Victor Jenkins went off his meds as well. You won't be able to interview him, but it also means he won't be testifying in person at the trial."

"I feel sorry for the man, but yes, all in all this is good news for our case."

"I'd say so. And hey, if you don't need me for anything else, I'll see you on Monday morning."

"Sure, I'll be headed home too. Say hi to Glenda for me."

Warren left the coffee maker ready to go for Monday morning and headed out his office door while whistling.

ASSISTANT DA PIA GONZALES HADN'T BEEN completely truthful with Gavin. While she had been at the halfway house to ask Victor Jenkins not to talk to the Defense, she also had a few questions of her own for Jenkins.

Gonzales had read the statement Jenkins had given about seeing Zander Hall on the night of the murders. One of the details Jenkins mentioned intrigued her. He had stated that he'd seen Hall switch the license plates. However, the plates that had been stolen off a similar SUV had never been recovered. Gonzales wondered if Jenkins knew what Hall had done with them.

She called a friend of hers, Jade Tulane. Jade was a police detective in the area where the stolen vehicle had been found. The two of them went into the alley where Hall had dumped the SUV and switched the plates. The alleyway had also been Jenkins' home while he lived on the streets.

"This is a long shot, Pia. Hall could have dumped those plates anywhere," Jade said.

"Yeah, but look around. No one ever sweeps this alley. They might be under all the trash that blows in here."

The two had been searching for ten minutes when Pia asked Jade to help her roll back a green dumpster that was against the wall and overflowing with trash. No one had emptied it as service had been cancelled a long time ago.

Pia kicked at yellowing sheets of newspaper and candy wrappers hoping to spot the glint of metal. Instead, she found an old leather knapsack that had been enclosed within a white trash bag. As she looked through the knapsack, Pia found a confusing mixture of items. There were covers from paperback novels, several balls of string, candy bar wrappers, a dog chew toy, and an unused sanitary napkin. There were also papers that had Victor Jenkins' name on them. One was an expired appointment card for the VA hospital in West Haven.

"Hey Pia, flip that bag over and look at what's sticking out of one of the compartments," Jade said.

Pia did so and saw the corner of a license plate. She smiled at Jade. "I think we might have struck gold here."

WARREN WAS IN A FINE MOOD AS HE ENTERED THE courtroom on Monday morning. He'd had a great weekend with his family, and it looked like he was on the verge of winning another case. His disposition soured when he was informed that new evidence had been uncovered. When he found out what that evidence was, he knew all was lost.

Warren met with Zander Hall in private minutes before the trial was to resume.

"They found a partial of your left thumbprint and the print of your right index finger on one of the license plates that was on the vehicle believed to have been at the scene of the murders, Zander. They were recovered from the alley where the stolen SUV was abandoned. As you can imagine, that will shatter any reasonable doubts about you the jury may have had."

"The license plates? That doesn't make sense. It's been weeks. How could my prints still be on them with all the rain and snow we've had?"

Warren sighed. Hall had all but admitted his guilt. An innocent man would have said it was impossible for his prints to have been on the license plates. Hall was only confused by how they could *still* be on the plates.

"You weren't alone in that alley. There was a homeless man living there. He saw you remove the plates, then for some reason he gathered them up and kept them in a knapsack, along with other miscellaneous items. The man suffers from schizophrenia."

Hall paced about the small room they were in with his lumbering gait. When he stopped, he had a question for Warren.

"Were the homeless guy's prints on the plates too?"

"Yes."

Hall smiled. "All right, then say he did the murders."

"That still wouldn't explain how your prints got on the plates."

"Shit, you're right."

Warren let out a long slow breath. "I'll do my best to negate this evidence, but you should be prepared for the worst."

"Fuck that! You do whatever you have to do, Blake, but make sure I'm found not guilty—or else."

"I don't like being threatened. It also does you no good to antagonize me."

Hall moved in close to Warren and got in his face. "Understand something, asshole. If I'm found guilty, I'll have nothing left to lose. There's no death penalty in this state and they can only lock me up once, no matter how many I kill."

Warren took a step back as he prepared to defend himself. Hall looked angry enough to strike him. If it happened, he wouldn't be the first lawyer assaulted by his own client.

There was a knock on the door, then Gavin stuck his head in the room. "Let's go, guys. The judge will be entering the courtroom any minute."

Warren nodded at Gavin, then gestured for Hall to leave the room first. Outside in the corridor were two sheriff's deputies. Warren guessed they were there to keep an eye on Hall. Hall had been out on bail and free to return home each night after the trial. Warren assumed that Hall's bail had been revoked and the deputies were there to see that he didn't make a break for it.

THINGS ONLY GOT WORSE AS THE DAY WENT ON. THE change in the jury's demeanor was startling after the new evidence was placed before them. Finding Hall's fingerprints on those license plates sealed his fate.

The jurors retired to the jury room shortly after the lunch break. When word came an hour later that they had reached a verdict, there was little doubt what it would be.

Zander Hall was found guilty of all charges, including one count of first-degree murder in the death of Douglas Stanton and second-degree murder for Mariana Hall. Sentencing would occur at a later date. It would likely result in Hall being behind bars for the rest of his life.

As he was being cuffed to be led away, Hall locked eyes with Warren Blake. "You're a dead man."

Warren felt a cold chill ripple along his spine at the utter conviction behind Hall's words.

"It was just a threat, Warren," Gavin said. "That big son of a bitch will never see the light of day again."

"Yeah, and I lost the case."

"Let me buy you a drink when we get out of here."

"Thanks, but I'll have to pass." Warren closed up

his briefcase. "I guess I should go talk to the reporters and get it over with."

"Good luck with those jackals."

"They're just doing their job; we're all just doing our jobs."

W<small>ARREN ARRIVED AT HIS OFFICE AT CLOSING TIME AND</small> found it nearly deserted. His office manager was there and gave him a look of commiseration. She was an older woman named Mrs. Simpson who had been with Warren for many years. Mrs. Simpson was gathering her things as she prepared to leave for the day.

There was also a young clerk present. His name was James Washington. James was a college student who wanted to be a lawyer. He had met Tanner and Sara two years earlier and been of help to them. To repay him, Sara had asked her father to hire James.

James enjoyed the work and was getting practical experience that would help him once he passed the bar exam. Warren had taken a liking to the young black man and wasn't surprised to see him working later than the other clerks.

"I heard you had a tough day, boss," James said.

Warren answered him as he settled behind his desk. "That's an understatement, but it happens. Let it be a lesson to you. Don't ever assume you have one in the win column until the trial is over."

"Will you appeal?"

"I'm sure the client will, but I won't be defending him. I've had enough of Zander Hall."

"The guy did seem like a jerk. He called all the women here honey, even Mrs. Simpson."

"I'm happy to be free of the case. Why don't you go home, James? I'm sure you've earned your pay."

"I was just going over what I had to do tomorrow, the way you taught me."

Warren smiled at him. "You're going to make a fine lawyer."

"I've still got four more years of study, but I'll get there."

"Have a good night," Warren said.

James sent him a wave and left the office. Warren swiveled his chair around and stared out the window. Just that morning he'd been certain he was headed toward another victory in the courtroom. Fate had other plans.

When he heard someone enter the office behind him, he thought it was James coming back in. He swiveled his chair around and found a tall, buxom woman in a red dress staring at him. She was not an attractive woman, despite the long blonde hair and full breasts. She had a large nose, beady eyes, and a fleshy face that had too much makeup caked on it.

When *she* spoke in a deep voice, Warren realized he was looking at a man in drag.

"Warren Blake?"

"That's right."

The cross-dresser removed a gun from the large purse he was carrying. It had a sound suppressor screwed onto the end of it.

"You shouldn't have lost the case, shyster."

The man raised the gun and took aim at Warren's chest.

7

CLOSE CALL

SARA AND TANNER WERE AT WARREN'S HOUSE IN Connecticut waiting for her father's return. They had heard what went on at the trial and knew he had lost the case.

They stood in the home's dining room, which was decorated to celebrate Lucas's first birthday. There were colorful balloons throughout the room and a pile of gaily wrapped gifts were on a table. In the kitchen was a birthday cake in the shape of a horse, as Lucas loved horses.

The guest of honor was lying in a playpen in the home's living room beside his cousin Emily. Both children napped after a day spent playing.

"I feel bad for Daddy, but it sounds like it's a good thing that Zander Hall is off the streets," Sara said.

"Hall may have killed his wife and her lover, but

someone else eliminated his alibi witnesses. Even the police admit he couldn't have been responsible for the deaths or that woman's disappearance."

"Maybe Hall will cut a deal for a lighter sentence and reveal who he hired to commit those murders."

"That's usually how it works," Tanner agreed.

The housekeeper, Mrs. Johnson, entered the room and began setting the table. She had been with Warren for twelve years, was about his age, and lived in the home. Mrs. Johnson had a lovely face and had trimmed down over the last year as she'd taken up jogging. She was a widow who had lost her husband while only in her thirties. Warren often said that he didn't know what he would do if he didn't have her. It was Mrs. Johnson who maintained the house and kept him organized. Sara helped her set the table.

"Have you heard from Daddy?"

"Yes. He called earlier and said he expected to be home a little late. He has to pick up his car from the dealership."

"That's okay. As tired as Lucas is, I don't think he'll be waking from his nap for some time."

"It's nice having children in the house, Sara, and your father adores them."

"I'm sorry that Daddy lost his case. At least he has a celebration to come home to. Maybe it will cheer him up."

"I'm sure it will," Mrs. Johnson agreed. "Thank

you for helping, now I need to get back to the kitchen to check on dinner."

Sara turned back to Tanner to see that he had a thoughtful expression. "What's on your mind?"

"I was thinking about Zander Hall's accomplice. He or she is still out there."

"There's always the possibility that Hall's witnesses really did die and go missing because of accidents."

"Maybe," Tanner said, but he didn't sound convinced.

WARREN THRUST HIS HANDS UP IN FRONT OF HIM IN A futile gesture to stop the bullet he was certain would end his life. The gun fired and the slug buried itself in his desk as the shooter was jostled.

James had come back, seen the "woman" pointing a gun at his boss, and rushed into the room to push down on the assassin's gun arm before attempting to wrest the weapon away.

Warren jumped to his feet and ran around the desk to help James. Before he could join the fray, James was shoved backwards into him. The two men fell to the floor at the side of the desk as the cross-dresser tore the wig off his head. During his struggle with James the wig had gone askew and blocked his vision. The man shouted at James.

"You wanted to be a hero, kid? Now you're going to be a dead hero."

"FBI! Drop the gun!"

Those words came from Jake Garner. He had arrived at the office to give Warren a lift to the car dealership where his vehicle was being serviced. When he heard the shot and the sounds of a struggle, he had taken out his weapon and rushed along the corridor to reach Warren's office.

The shooter jerked his head around and saw that Jake had his gun pointed at him. His own gun was still aimed at James and Warren.

"If you shoot me, I'll shoot them," the man said.

Jake moved into the room in two long strides and pressed the barrel of his weapon against the man's head.

"You have three seconds to put down that gun. One...two..."

The gun made a thud as it hit the carpet. Moments later, Jake had the shooter on the floor with his wrists bound behind him by a belt. Jake had to use his belt instead of handcuffs. He carried a weapon when off duty, but not handcuffs.

James was grinning at him. "You saved our lives, Agent Garner."

Warren clapped James on the shoulder. "And you

saved mine. If you hadn't returned when you did that… man, would have killed me."

"I remembered hearing that your car was in the shop; I came back to see if you needed a ride home."

"That's why I'm here," Jake said, as he took out his phone to call the police.

WARREN AND JAKE DIDN'T ARRIVE HOME FOR HOURS, as the shooting incident and the attempted murders had to be investigated and they were interviewed by police detectives. Jennifer, Sara, and Tanner met them at the door as they entered the house. Sara went to her father as Jennifer greeted her husband.

"You had a close call, Daddy."

"That's an understatement. I nearly died twice. Thank God James and Jake were there."

Jake smiled. "You might want to give that young man a raise."

"A raise?" Warren said. "Hell, I'll be paying his way through law school."

"What about the man who tried to kill you?" Tanner asked. "Was it someone you knew?"

"I'd never seen him before. He told the detectives that he was hired over the internet to kill me. Someone paid him five thousand dollars."

"My God, Daddy," Jennifer said. "Do they know who it is that hired him?"

"It was anonymous, but I'm certain Zander Hall was behind it. The last thing the man said to me was that I was a dead man. He also threatened me during the trial."

"You need to hire a bodyguard, Daddy. Better yet, two of them, or have the police protect you," Sara said.

"Hall is behind bars, honey. He won't be hiring any more third-rate killers to go after me."

"Warren," Tanner said, "Hall might have an accomplice, the same person who disposed of his alibi witnesses."

The truth of that struck Warren, causing him to hang his head. "I need a drink."

The sound of a car arriving in the driveway could be heard. Tanner moved toward the door and used one of the decorative glass panels on the side of it to look out.

"It's Nina."

Tanner opened the door for Nina. She rushed inside and began looking Warren over, as if she were checking him for injuries.

"Oh my God. Did someone really try to kill you?"

"Yes, but I'm unharmed."

"Do the police know what was behind it?"

"I think it was Zander Hall wanting revenge on me because I lost his case."

Nina appeared disgusted. "I'm sorry you lost, Warren, but I'm so glad that man is behind bars."

Hall was locked away. Tanner knew it meant he had nothing to lose by having Warren or anyone else killed he thought had wronged him. He gestured for Jake to step aside so that they could talk in private.

"What's up?" Jake said.

"If Hall was bold enough to hire someone to kill Warren, he might also go after the judge or the jurors. You might want to tell the cops to keep an eye on all of them."

"I guess it's possible, but he'd have no way of knowing who the jurors are."

"There are ways. And don't forget, he's got at least one accomplice out there. Hall is also rich enough to pay for a small army of killers."

"All right, I'll make certain the police are aware of the threat."

"I'm going to keep watch here tonight, just in case."

"You think that's necessary?"

"It sounds like the first hitter was a clown, the next one may not be."

Jake nodded. "You take first watch and I'll relieve you at three a.m."

Mrs. Johnson entered the foyer. She was carrying Lucas using her right arm and held Emily's hand.

"The birthday boy has woken up."

Warren took Lucas from Mrs. Johnson and gave his grandson a kiss. "Enough sad talk; let's celebrate."

Everyone savored a fine dinner then watched Lucas receive his gifts, but there was a pall over what should have been a joyous occasion. Warren had nearly died. Tanner couldn't help but wonder if the danger had ended, or if the threat was just beginning.

CYRUS DALY LEARNED OF THE FAILED ATTEMPT ON Warren Blake's life as he was sitting in a bar watching the news. There was also coverage of the trial and the new evidence that had sunk Hall's chances at an acquittal.

Before the trial had begun, Hall had made arrangements with Cyrus. He had given him a very simple set of instructions and access to enough money to carry them out.

"If Blake fails and I'm sent away, make sure that son of a bitch dies. Hire whoever you have to, but make sure that I can at least have the satisfaction of knowing he paid for losing the case."

"I could do the job."

"No Cyrus, hire someone. I have other plans for you. You'll have a chance to enjoy yourself by arranging accidents and disappearances."

Cyrus smiled. "Who will I be going after?"

"I don't know their names and probably never will, but I know what they'll be called."

"What's that?"

"A jury. If I'm convicted, start picking those fuckers off one by one. And take your time. The cops will catch on, but they can't protect them forever. If you're careful, you should have a lot of fun."

"That will be a blast, and tricky, but hey, Zander. You won't go to prison. That guy Blake knows his stuff."

"He'd better," Zander Hall had said.

Cyrus returned from the memory in time to see that the man he'd been following was saying goodbye to his friends as he prepared to leave the bar. He was a young man who had gone prematurely bald. The baldness only tended to emphasize his chiseled features. Until a few hours ago, he had been the foreman at the trial of Zander Hall.

Cyrus left a tip for the bartender and slipped off his stool. He had prey to follow and a disappearance to arrange.

A FACE WITHOUT A NAME

Warren learned about the missing jury foreman three days later. Apparently, the man had disappeared while walking home from a neighborhood bar.

The cross-dresser who had tried to kill Warren was no help in tracking down the person who'd hired him. His payment had arrived in a P.O. Box in the form of fifty, one-hundred-dollar bills. The money was recovered from the shooter's apartment; the only prints on it were his own.

Zander Hall had hired a new attorney who seemed an unlikely choice to Warren. The lawyer's name was Nick Medina. Medina had a horrible reputation and had never filed an appeal or defended anyone in a criminal case. His specialty was filing frivolous lawsuits. He'd only recently begun practicing law in Connecticut after having been disbarred in Florida, Maryland, and New Jersey. What Warren didn't understand is that Medina was the perfect man for what Hall had in mind.

HALL MET WITH HIS NEW ATTORNEY AFTER HAVING spent a day in solitary confinement. The authorities believed he was behind the attempted murder of Warren Blake but proving it was another matter. Detectives investigating the disappearance of the jury foreman had visited Hall. He smiled at them and asked a question.

"What are you going to do if I admit I had that bald asshole killed, arrest me for murder and lock me away? I'm already locked up."

One of the cops had leaned in and whispered to Hall. "There's doing time, and then there's doing hard time. You don't want to do hard time, old man."

Hall had cursed at him while insulting his mother. When he left them, Hall was shoved into solitary confinement.

NICK MEDINA WAS A SMALL MAN WHO LOOKED nothing like what he was, a sleaze ball. Medina was handsome, wore a trim mustache, and dressed in expensive suits. He had the look of a high-priced lawyer and the morals of a lowlife punk.

Medina smiled at his client. "I heard they threw you in the hole."

"Yeah. It was nice and peaceful in there. Do you have a message for me?"

"Our mutual friend wants you to know that he's hard at work," Medina said, referring to Cyrus Daly, although he'd never met Cyrus in person.

Hall appeared pleased by that news. It meant that Cyrus was keeping with the plan. He had given his friend access to a lot of money. Hall had thought there was a fifty-fifty chance that Cyrus would have taken the funds for himself, even if he was already being well-compensated.

"Stay in touch with him by email like we set it up," Hall told Medina. "When there's news, come and tell me. It's all I've got to look forward to in here. And oh yeah, you're using a burner phone to check the emails, right?"

"Absolutely. I don't want there to be any way this can be traced back to me."

"You don't even know what *this* is."

"I can guess what you're doing, Hall. I don't think it's ever been done before. You've got to know that the authorities are going to do everything they can to get you to talk and tell them about our friend."

"I won't say shit, and all you've got is an email address."

"I would never help them in any event. Besides, I'm protected from saying anything due to Attorney-Client privilege."

"I thought that didn't count if you knew about a crime."

"What crime? All I do is deliver messages back and forth."

Hall laughed. "I see I hired the right man. I have a new message for our friend. Tell him to up the stakes. He'll know what I mean."

"If that means what I think, expect to spend more time in solitary confinement."

Hall waved that off. "My old man used to lock me in a trunk when I was a kid. Once he left me in there for two days. Believe me, they can't do anything in here to me that I haven't already been through worse."

Medina grimaced as he imagined being confined inside a lightless, tight space for days. It's a wonder Hall hadn't gone mad. He told his client that he would relay the message by leaving an unsent email message in a draft folder. Medina stood and went to the door. He was about to tell the guard that he was ready to leave when he decided to quench his curiosity.

"Whatever became of your father? Was he arrested for child abuse?"

"No. I never told anyone what he did to me until later."

"Is he still living?"

Hall's smile was chilling. "He stopped living a long time ago."

"I see," Medina said.

"Make sure you give our friend that message."

"Absolutely," Medina said. He had no intention of failing in his duties. He didn't want to wind up on Hall's kill list the way his last lawyer had.

ANOTHER WEEK PASSED AND ANOTHER OF THE JURORS was visited by misfortune. Her name was Robin Vicenti. She died of an overdose after it was assumed that she had inadvertently taken too much of her heart medicine. Because she had served on Hall's jury, homicide detectives had investigated the death. They found no evidence of a break-in or foul play.

Vicenti had a small bruise on one wrist, but it was thought to be too minor to jump to the conclusion that she had struggled with someone.

Robin Vicenti had been found lying in bed looking peaceful, with nothing out of place or disturbed.

One day after her demise was ruled Death by Medical Misadventure, another juror went missing. His name was Abel Samuels. Mr. Samuels rode the subway to and from his job as a shoe salesman and was captured on video as he passed through a turnstile while on his way home from work. He never arrived there. The next day someone wearing a hood and dark sunglasses used Samuels' credit card at a Walmart in the Bronx. They had used it to purchase a book on how to commit suicide along with a sharp knife.

The unidentified man was about Samuels' size and couldn't be ruled out as being the former juror. The case was sent to the Missing Persons Division where it joined thousands of other unsolved disappearances, many concerning teens and young children.

Warren Blake enjoyed the protection of the police for several days after the attempt on his life. When there were no further signs that he was a target, the protection was dropped. Both Jennifer and Sara insisted that their father continue to take precautions. Warren hired a pair of bodyguards who followed him around for a week. It was a week in which he did nothing but go to the office and return home; it lessened the opportunities for an attack.

Despite learning that two of the jurors in his last case had gone missing while another had died suddenly, Warren wasn't ready to attribute the events to Zander Hall. After all, Hall was behind bars and had received no visitors other than his new lawyer.

Warren still believed that Hall had been the instigator behind the attempt on his life. He just assumed that having failed and been suspected of the crime that Hall wouldn't try to have him killed again. If the man had any hope of winning an appeal or not being sentenced to life in prison, it would be wise for him to not heap suspicion upon himself.

Tanner and Sara stayed with Warren longer than they had planned to. They were both concerned that the threat against him wasn't over.

When Zander Hall was handed down a sentence of life plus thirty years without the possibility of parole, Tanner knew that Hall now truly had nothing to lose. He and Sara sat down with Warren and expressed their concerns.

"I UNDERSTAND THAT YOU'RE WORRIED ABOUT ME, honey, but I really think the threat is over," Warren told Sara. They were seated together in the living room at the house in Connecticut. "If it was Hall who hired that man who tried to kill me in my office, he's obviously given up. After all, that was over a week ago."

"I can tell you from experience that it can take time to hire an assassin," Tanner said. "Hall might have instructed whoever is helping him to find a real professional, and not someone like the clown who was in your office."

"Clown? That clown nearly killed me."

"You were seated in your office in front of a window. If I'd had the contract, I would have used a rifle and shot you from half a mile away. Other pros might do the same."

Warren looked over at the bay windows. "Is that why the drapes are drawn?"

"Yes, Daddy. We think you're still at risk."

"The police are investigating the disappearances of the jurors, but that woman died from taking too much medicine. There's no reason to think that Hall was behind that."

"Are you forgetting what happened to his alibi witnesses?" Sara asked. "Zander Hall has a partner, someone who's willing to do his dirty work or hire it out. Until we find that person, you're not safe."

"You've been investigating?"

"Yes, and so has Jake. Tanner also has people looking into it; they're people who can dig in places Jake and I can't."

Warren looked at Tanner with surprise registering on his face. "You have people? I thought you always worked alone."

"The world becomes more complicated every day. I sometimes need assistance. The people I have looking into this are good at what they do."

"Who are they?" Warren asked.

MICHAEL AND KATE BARLOW WERE IN A BAR IN Manhattan waiting to meet someone who had information for them. When the young, raven-haired beauty arrived, every male head in the room turned to look at her with desire, while many of the women stared at her in envy.

Her name was Joy. Years earlier Michael and Kate had used her when they were investigating Tanner for Ordnance Inc. Joy had been a stripper at Johnny R's. She had gotten close enough to Tanner to pluck a loose hair off his shoulder so that the Barlows would have his DNA. Tanner later uncovered the Barlows' connection to Ordnance Inc. The couple had never disclosed to him that Joy had been involved.

Currently, Joy was working as a prostitute in a brothel. Her annual compensation was somewhere in the mid-six-figures.

The brothel was located inside a hotel. It took up an entire floor and catered to a rich clientele. The owners were two sisters who were former prostitutes from Las Vegas. Thirty-five percent of everything they made went to the Giacconi Family. In return, they were allowed to operate and didn't have to worry about the law.

Two years earlier a five-man team had robbed the sisters. Joe Pullo was informed and handed the problem over to Bosco, who assigned it to Rico Nazario and his crew. A short time later, the five men were dead, the money was returned, and Pullo gifted the sisters twenty thousand dollars for their trouble. The twenty thousand had been part of seventy-four thousand that had been found in the robbery crew's possession at the time Rico and his men caught up to them. It had been money they had accumulated by committing other robberies.

Those other heists had been done outside Joe Pullo's territory and had gone unavenged. The Giacconis were not ones to let a bad deed go unpunished.

Joy's figure was displayed well by the short skirt and skimpy top she wore. Her long black hair hung down her back and shimmered in the overhead lighting. When she reached the Barlows' table, she sat close to Michael and sent him a bright smile.

"You're as handsome as I remember, Michael."

"He's also still married," Kate said.

Joy laughed. "Are you afraid I'll steal him away?"

"No, you might borrow him without asking, though."

"I'm a one-woman man," Michael said. He slid an envelope over to Joy. It contained a thousand dollars. Joy did nothing for anyone unless she was being paid.

A female bartender asked Joy if she wanted a drink or to place a lunch order. Joy ordered two apple martinis while the Barlows had more of the red wine they were drinking.

"Two martinis?" Kate asked.

"You're paying, right?"

"Yes."

"I want to get my money's worth. Besides, I love apple martinis."

Once they had their drinks, Joy downed a martini in a matter of moments, then began sipping her second one.

Michael started things off. "Let's get down to business. Joy, you said on the phone that you remember Zander Hall visited the brothel with another man sometimes. Give us a description."

"He was a little guy, and thin. He was probably about fifty, because he had lines around his eyes, but he looked younger and had these rosy cheeks. I thought it was makeup at first because of how red they were. And oh yeah, his eyes are a really bright blue."

"Did he have an accent, tattoos, anything that might distinguish him further?"

"No, nothing like that."

"Did you ever hear his name?" Kate asked?

"Probably, but who remembers the name of a john?"

"Are you saying you slept with the man?"

"That's what I was paid to do, Kate. I made more than most people make in a week to do it and I don't think the guy lasted three minutes. Let me tell you, hooking is much easier work than stripping."

"I'll have to take your word for that; I've never been a whore."

"That's not what I hear. You and Michael sell yourselves all the time. We're not unalike, Kate. We just supply different services."

Michael cleared his throat. He could see that his wife was growing angry and didn't want the conversation to devolve into an argument. He asked Joy a question to get things back on track.

"When was the last time you saw Zander Hall's friend?"

"A few weeks before the trial started. Hall was with him then too."

"Does the guy visit the brothel often?"

"Not really. I have some clients that see me once

a week. I've only seen the guy with the red cheeks a few times."

"If you ever see him again, please let us know; we'll make it worth your while."

"I'll be sure to call. I enjoy talking to you, Michael."

"I bet you do," Kate said. "Every time you hear from us you get paid."

Joy stood. "So long, Kate." Before leaving, she caressed Michael's cheek. "I hope to hear from you."

"Michael isn't calling you; you're to call us if you come across Hall's friend," Kate said.

"I can think of a reason Michael might call me," Joy said, smiling at Michael. Before Kate could respond, Joy turned away and sauntered out of the bar. Her exit noted by delighted males and relieved females.

Michael had refrained from watching Joy but was aware that Kate was staring at him. He met her eyes.

"She was only flirting with me because she knows it irks you."

Kate stared back at him, grumbled something unintelligible, then got up and headed towards the restrooms. Michael groaned. It was going to be a long day.

9

SCREAMFEST

It was only the second day of the season at Great Escapades Amusement Park but already the park was crowded with winter-weary fun seekers.

One of those in attendance was a thirty-two-year-old man named Larry Huckel. Huckel had been a juror at the Zander Hall murder trial. He was spending the day with his girlfriend and was enjoying the warm spring weather.

Larry Huckel had always loved amusement parks and went to them whenever he had the time. He was especially fond of roller coasters, and the scarier they were the better. The one he was standing in line for was a monster named Screamfest. It stood four hundred and fifty feet high and could propel you along at over a hundred miles an hour. Larry's girlfriend, Colleen, was nervous about going on it.

97

"It'll be great; you'll love it. I must have ridden it a dozen times last year."

"I just hope I don't throw up," Colleen said.

Their turn to board the ride came a few minutes later. Larry was delighted to find that they would have seats at the very front of Screamfest. Larry and Colleen settled in their seats and pulled down their safety restraints. Screamfest's restraints worked using hydraulic fluid and a piston. The fluid flowed through tubes and into a cylinder that was monitored by a check valve. As the restraint is pulled down and into place, hydraulic fluid gathered behind the piston. The check valve prohibited the flow of the fluid, so the restraint was incapable of releasing and moving up during the ride. Once the roller coaster returned to the station, it connected with electrical contacts that signaled the system to redirect the fluid so that the piston could move. The restraint could then be pushed up and out of the way, allowing the ride's patrons the freedom to stand.

However, in an emergency situation, park employees could use a special power pack to signal the flow of the hydraulic fluid, allowing the restraint bar to be moved. Cyrus Daly was aware of that and intended to put the knowledge to malevolent use.

CYRUS HAD BEEN PLANNING ON HOW TO KILL THE jurors when the trial was still underway. He hadn't wanted Hall to be found guilty, but every cloud had a silver lining. The jury hadn't been sequestered and was allowed to return home each night. Once the trial started and the jury had been selected, it had been a simple thing for Cyrus to follow them.

Jurors in murder trials were afforded free parking in the courthouse's fenced-in lot. Each parking space had a number stenciled on it. It was the same number as the courtroom the case was being held in. Cyrus had staked out the roof of a nearby building and used a camera with a powerful zoom lens to watch the jurors arrive for court. Once he had their pictures and knew what they were driving, he hired a hooker to distract the lot attendant while he slipped in over the fence. GPS trackers were attached to the undercarriage of each vehicle and allowed Cyrus to know their home addresses.

Several of the jurors didn't drive. It took longer to identify them. One such juror had been the shoe salesman, Abel Samuels. Cyrus had to follow him on foot and in the subway. Samuels was a pipe smoker who had a habit of stopping at a tobacco shop on his way home. He would do so on Fridays.

Cyrus left the subway at a run and headed to the tobacco shop. While donning a mask he robbed the shopkeeper after using a short club to knock the man out. When Samuels entered the store minutes later, the security camera was off, and Cyrus was waiting for him. He herded Samuels into a back room and out a rear door that opened onto an alley.

Samuels grunted as he too was clubbed. Cyrus had hit him just hard enough to stun him and make him easier to handle. While prodding Samuels with a gun, Cyrus led the staggering man over to a car parked near a row of trash cans. Cyrus opened the trunk of his rented car, clubbed Samuels again, and shoved him inside. Two more blows from the club assured him that Samuels wouldn't make a peep during the ride.

Cyrus removed the mask as he was opening the car to climb in and heard a door open on one of the other shops. A young woman with colorful tattoos on her arms stepped out carrying a bag of garbage. She barely gave Cyrus a glance. Even from where he was, he could hear the thump of the vintage heavy metal music coming through the earbuds she was wearing.

Cyrus climbed into the car and drove off. When the shopkeeper revived his senses, he called the police and reported the robbery. Days later when he saw the face of his customer, Abel Samuels, on the news, it didn't occur to him that Samuels' disappearance could be related to his robbery.

As for Samuels, his fate was a cruel one. Cyrus loved creating "accidents." Those he killed in such a manner were the lucky ones. The men and women he had caused to go missing over the years were also dead, but they had suffered before that sweet release was granted.

Cyrus Daly was a sadist. Giving pain to others gave him pleasure. He tortured Abel Samuels for days before he killed him, as he had done with the bald jury foreman, and Hall's alibi witness, Elsa Kaplan. His new target was Larry Huckel. Larry's death would be swift and dramatic.

AFTER LEARNING WHERE HUCKEL LIVED, CYRUS HAD broken into his home and went through his belongings. He discovered that Huckel had a season pass to the amusement park. After seeing a date circled on the calendar in the kitchen with the name of the theme park written down, Cyrus's evil mind formed a plan. In truth, it was an idea he had been nurturing for years but never got around to implementing. It would be the best accidental death he'd ever arranged.

Although he hadn't yet known if Hall would be found guilty, it didn't matter. He would have killed

Larry Huckel in any event. What he had in mind was too good to let go.

He needed help to pull it off. That assistance came from a man whose services he had used before. The guy was a genius when it came to electronics or anything computer related. The best thing about him was that he never asked any nosy questions. All he cared about was creating what you wanted, and of course, money.

Cyrus was inside the amusement park and dressed like one of the ride attendants with a red jacket and a matching cap. One of the real workers, a younger man with a crewcut asked him his name. Cyrus gave him the name that matched his phony employee ID.

"I've never seen you before, but I guess you're one of the new people, hmm?"

"That's right. I was hired over the winter."

"How do you like it so far?"

"It's exciting."

The other man smiled. "We'll see how you feel once you've been here a few weeks."

As Larry Huckel and his girlfriend, Colleen, climbed into their seats, Cyrus made sure he was the one to check their restraints. While doing so, he attached a small box to the side of the housing of Larry's restraint. It matched the housing's bright blue color and secured itself magnetically.

Colleen looked at Cyrus and asked a question. "How scary is this ride?"

Cyrus grinned at her. "More than you can imagine."

The ride began moments later. As it picked up speed while rocketing along its track, Cyrus reached into his pocket and took out what looked like a key fob for a car. When he pushed the button on it, a red light blinked twice.

As the ride reached its apex it slowed before heading toward a plunging section of track. When it went downward at great speed without anything bad happening, Cyrus wondered if the device he had was working properly. It was then he remembered that the light on the key fob should have blinked green, not red. He pressed the button again, sending out a signal as the ride sped along a length of track directly overhead.

He was rewarded by seeing a green flashing light. That indicated that an electrical signal had been sent. The hydraulic fluid in Larry Huckel's restraint was draining into a different tube and releasing the piston that held it in place.

Once again, the ride climbed in preparation of taking another stomach-flipping descent in which the ride's participants would be hanging upside down. When it sped along the track, several women screamed as a body was ejected from the ride.

Larry Huckel died as a result of falling four hundred and seventeen feet to the ground. Before leaving the amusement park, Cyrus removed the device that had been used to override the check valve on Huckel's seat restraint.

Cyrus drove home while humming to himself. When he checked his laptop, he saw that there was more good news. The second hit man he had hired to eliminate Warren Blake had arrived in Connecticut.

Cyrus composed a quick email which he would leave in the draft folder of the account for Nick Medina to read and relay to Hall. It read: Four down, and #1 should be next.

Cyrus smiled as he sat back in his seat. By the time he and Hall were through, every jury in the country would think twice before handing down a guilty verdict. He wondered how many more he'd have to kill before the cops began guarding the rest of the jurors 24/7, or maybe they would even offer to place them in something like the Witness Protection Program.

Larry Huckel's death might do it, or maybe it wouldn't. An investigation should reach the conclusion that Huckel died as the result of a freak accident.

Warren Blake's death wouldn't look like an accident. The man Cyrus had hired to kill him was an ex-military contractor who had a reputation of being a killer of skill and ability. He had cost Cyrus fifty thousand dollars to hire. Warren Blake could run, but he wouldn't be able to hide, not forever.

Cyrus leaned back, closed his eyes, and laughed as he recalled the sound Larry Huckel's body made as it hit the ground.

OPPOSITE DAY

ALTHOUGH LARRY HUCKEL'S DEATH WAS CLASSIFIED AS an accident, Warren Blake wasn't willing to bet his life on it. Huckel was the fourth of Hall's former jurors to die or go missing and even the police had to admit it appeared suspicious. That was in private conversations. Officially, they steadfastly maintained that the deaths and disappearances plaguing the jurors was a string of unfortunate happenstance. They were going to increase patrols around the remaining jurors, Warren, and the judge in the case, but they weren't willing to shell out overtime to guard everyone twenty-four hours a day. Doing so would also signal that they believed the jurors were targets of a killer.

If it became known that people serving as jurors in murder cases could be placing themselves at risk, many trials might end with a not guilty verdict, despite the evidence of guilt presented. After all, if someone is on trial for murder, there's an even chance they're guilty. If they killed once, why not kill again? Murderers have served short sentences and been released. Even cop killers have been paroled. No one serving on a jury would want to find someone guilty of murder then spend the rest of their lives looking over their shoulders.

Most of Hall's remaining jurors took matters into their own hands and left the area. Warren intended to do the same thing and Sara agreed. Why make it easy for Hall's unknown partner to find him?

She wanted her father to travel to Texas with them and stay at the ranch. Blake refused. He didn't want to risk attracting trouble to their home.

"Cody and I can protect you there; we have excellent security in place."

"You also have my grandson. I won't risk bringing trouble around him."

"Where will you go?"

"I know you were only about ten the last time you saw him, but do you remember my old law professor, Bill Evans?"

"Uncle Bill? Of course, I remember him. He taught me how to clean fish."

"You'll recall his cabin too then, the one in Maine.

Bill left it to me in his will years ago. It's quite literally in the middle of nowhere. The nearest road is six miles away and the closest town is even farther."

"You intend to walk in from the road?" Tanner asked. His father-in-law was in good shape for his age, but he didn't see the man taking a six-mile hike through woodlands while carrying supplies on his back.

"I'll fly myself there in my plane. Bill taught Sara how to clean fish, but he taught me to fly. There's a landing strip and a hangar near the cabin. Once I'm there, no one will be able to find me."

Sara was nodding. "I like it. And while you're there, Jake and I will be working to find Hall's accomplice. Once we've identified him it will be safe for you to come back."

"Has there been any progress?" Warren asked.

"I was given a description of a small man with red cheeks and bright blue eyes," Tanner said. "Have you ever seen Hall with anyone like that?"

"No, but other than a courtroom I've only met with Zander inside my office."

"When are you planning to leave, Daddy?"

"Tomorrow. I've asked Lydia, Mrs. Johnson, to buy the things I'll need for my trip. She's out gathering them up now," Warren said as he stood. "I'm going up to pack clothes for the trip. I'll take a fishing rod along as well; I'm sure the fishing is still good up there."

Warren left the room and Sara reached over and took Tanner's hand. "I want you to go with Daddy. Will you do it?"

"I could, but I was planning on looking for Hall's accomplice."

"Jake and I can handle that, but I'd feel better if I knew you were protecting Daddy."

"Protecting people isn't exactly my specialty."

"I know you've been trained to take lives not save them, but I also know that there's no one better at survival than you. Cody... I'm worried about my father. Please say that you'll keep him safe."

Tanner gave her hand a squeeze. "I'll go, and I promise I won't let anything happen to him."

Sara grinned. "Thank you. That takes a load off my mind."

"I'll call Kate and Michael and tell them that they're to report to you if they uncover anything else."

"Do you think they will?"

"Yeah. They'll keep digging until they find Hall's friend. Kate and Michael are relentless when they're working."

"I wanted to strangle them when I heard what they had done to your family's graves, but now I'm glad you didn't kill them."

"No, instead I hired them, and now I'll be working hard to keep someone alive. If there was such a thing as an assassin's union, I would probably be kicked out of it for conduct unbecoming a killer."

Sara laughed. "If there was a union, you'd be its president."

Tanner took out his phone. "I'm going to give Duke a call. There are a few supplies I want to take along to Maine. I'll drive into the city later and pick them up."

"Lucas and I will be staying at the penthouse while you're gone."

"That's good. No one should stay here in case someone comes to the house looking for your father, that includes Mrs. Johnson."

"I'll ask her to come to the penthouse with me."

"Good. She'll be able to help you with Lucas too."

Warren returned downstairs carrying a suitcase, which he sat by the door. When Sara told him that she wanted Tanner to join him at the cabin in Maine, Warren stared at Tanner.

"How do you feel about that?"

"I think it's a good idea. We don't know who might have been hired to kill you. If they're skilled, they might track you down in Maine."

"That seems unlikely."

"I could do it; others might be able to as well."

"I'm glad you weren't approached."

"I would have refused the contract… depending on how much was offered."

Sara slapped Tanner on the arm. "You would never take such a contract and you know it, even if you didn't know Daddy."

"That's because I'm a Tanner. Others in my profession don't live by a set of rules."

Warren offered Tanner his hand. "I admit I'll feel better having you along. Not only will it make the time up there less boring, but I know that I'll be safe if anyone finds me."

"I won't let anything happen to you. If someone tries to kill you it will be the last thing they ever do."

"Like fighting fire with fire?" Warren said.

Sara kissed Tanner. "It will be more like dousing a match with a fire hydrant. No one is better than my husband, no one."

Tanner gazed back at Sara, realizing he loved her more every day. Ten minutes later, he was out the door and headed to New York City. It was time to gear up and prepare for any attack.

A NAME TO GO WITH THE FACE

THE NEXT DAY, MICHAEL AND KATE BARLOW MET with Joy again in the same Manhattan bar they had gathered in recently. They were both tired as they had been tracking down and interviewing Hall's employees, asking if they had seen him in the presence of someone who matched Cyrus's description. Several had, but no one knew his name or his connection to Hall. Joy had called with news that she had additional information about Zander Hall's mysterious friend.

"I want more money."

Michael patted an envelope that was on the table. "It's right here."

Joy shook her head. "I want more money than that." She then squinted. "It's bright in here."

It wasn't that bright. Joy was high on something

and her pupils were dilated. She also appeared to have started drinking before the Barlows had arrived. Getting free drinks would not be a problem for a woman who looked like Joy.

"We'll pay more if what you have is worth it," Kate said.

"I saw him again. He was walking out of the hotel as I was coming to work."

"He had been with another of the women?" Michael asked.

Joy smiled at him. "I know, it's hard to believe, isn't it? You would think he would want to be with me again. But then, all men crave variety, right, Michael?"

"Cut the crap, Joy, and tell us what you have," Kate said.

"Are you jealous because Michael is attracted to me?"

"You're attractive, but my husband would never sleep with you. Michael is faithful. Besides, he has an aversion to venereal diseases."

Joy called Kate a bitch as she grabbed her purse and stood. "I can sell the information I have to a reporter. I know that this is the guy the police are looking for. He's not just Zander Hall's friend; he's also his accomplice. I bet the news will pay to have a picture of him."

"You have a photo?" Michael asked.

"I took it as he was getting into a cab. I also followed him." Joy laughed. "You should have seen the cabbie's face when I told him to follow the taxi in front of him. He thought I was joking."

"Sit down. We'll pay," Kate said.

"I want five thousand."

"We don't have that much," Michael said. "We're also working for someone else who will have to decide if they want to pay."

"Call them," Joy said, as she sat back down.

The day before, Tanner had informed the Barlows that Sara would be handling things while he was away. Michael sent her a text and explained the situation. Sara responded within minutes.

Pay her if you think it's worth it.

"Okay. Our employer will pay, but we have to know if what you have is any good. Let's see the photo."

Joy brought out her phone and showed the Barlows a photo of Cyrus Daly. It had been taken in profile and showed his left side. There was one rosy cheek and a brilliant blue eye below a head of wavy brown hair.

"I've seen better driver's license photos," Kate said.

"There's also his address. I know where you can find him. I might even know his name. I watched him take mail out of a mailbox in the lobby."

"Take the thousand in the envelope and we'll pay you the remainder tomorrow."

Joy shook her head. "Cash up front, or I walk."

Kate released a huff and stood. "I'll be right back, Michael. We have money in a safe deposit box near Midtown. I should be back in twenty minutes."

"Aren't you afraid of leaving me alone with your husband, Kate?"

"Michael knows better than to play with dirty things."

Joy narrowed her eyes. "Watch it, bitch, or I'll hold out for more money."

"Keep her here, Michael. I won't be long."

IT TOOK KATE THIRTY-ONE MINUTES TO GET THE money and return. When she entered the bar again, she saw that Joy was at a table with three young men dressed in suits. Two of them had wedding rings and all three were practically drooling over Joy.

Michael was where Kate had left him, he was checking the news on his phone.

"How did it go?"

"The bank was crowded, so it took longer than I thought. I see that Joy has managed to keep herself amused."

"Yeah. When I wouldn't play along with her flirting, she decided to make new friends."

Joy left her three male admirers and rejoined Michael and Kate. She was taking deliberate steps, aware that she was drunk.

"Do you have the money, Kate?"

Kate slid over a bank envelope that contained five thousand dollars.

"What's the address?"

Joy mentioned a building in the SoHo district.

"And the name?"

"According to the mailbox he emptied, his name is Cyrus Daly."

CYRUS HAD SPENT THE MORNING GATHERING THINGS to make his eventual exit from the city. Later in the day he was meeting with a man who would supply him with a set of primo fake IDs. He would have to pay twenty-two thousand dollars for them. It would include a California driver's license, a passport, and a bank account with a token hundred dollars in it.

He knew when he'd decided to help Hall carry out his plans for revenge that he was risking being arrested and tried for murder himself. That was okay. Unlike Hall, he had no intention of staying and taking his chances if things went south.

He could have left days ago, after Hall was locked away. Zander Hall had given him access to millions of dollars. Instead of hiring killers to go after Warren Blake, Cyrus could have kept it all and ignored his friend's wishes.

He couldn't do that. He could torture people for the sheer pleasure of it and murder without mercy, but he hadn't wanted to let down the only friend he had ever known. He was a nobody, but Hall had always treated him like he mattered.

Besides, he didn't need much money to live on. Then again, he had developed a taste for the good things in life by spending time with Hall. It was why he'd recently treated himself to a high-priced hooker instead of picking up a girl on the street as he usually did.

Larry Huckel's death at the amusement park grabbed the attention of reporters after they became aware that he was the fourth of the Zander Hall murder trial jurors to meet with misfortune. Even talk radio was abuzz with speculation that Hall had a partner who was getting revenge for him.

That was too bad. Cyrus had been hoping to kill at least one more before he had to stop, but with all the attention, that time had arrived.

Warren Blake was another matter altogether. Cyrus could stay after Blake until he was dead because he didn't need to risk himself to do so.

Zander had wanted Blake dead most of all. Cyrus was determined to see that his friend at least had the pleasure of knowing Blake had been killed while he rotted away in prison.

The new hit man he had hired said he was on Blake's tail and would kill him as soon as he got the chance. That was good. If he managed to slaughter the lawyer soon, Cyrus could leave the city for California and his new life. Then, after a year or so had passed and everyone forgot about the jurors in the Hall trial, Cyrus could fly into town and kill another one. It might take him a decade or more, but he figured he could get to all of them eventually. It would be his way of letting Zander know that he hadn't forgotten him.

Cyrus had been so lost in what to his warped mind were pleasant thoughts, that he nearly forgot to take precautions when returning home. The police were looking for Hall's accomplice; he didn't want to make it easy for them to grab him up if they somehow found him.

He had installed hidden cameras outside his apartment door and in the apartment too. He leaned back against the outer wall of a coffee shop that was a block from his home and accessed the cameras on his phone.

"Son of a bitch," Cyrus whispered. There were two men inside his apartment waiting for him to arrive. They might be cops, but Cyrus was guessing it was more likely Feds. It was plain to see by the disarray in the apartment that it had been searched. He was burned.

THE TWO MEN INSIDE CYRUS'S APARTMENT WERE federal agents. After getting Cyrus's name and address from the Barlows, Sara had told Jake Garner about it then had Michael and Kate send the information to Jake anonymously, along with a story that would leave Joy out of it.

Jake contacted the police, and a judge signed off on a search warrant. As much as he had wanted to get involved, Jake had handed the case off to his colleagues. He was the son-in-law of a victim and didn't want to give a defense attorney any ammunition to throw out the case or suggest that Jake had planted evidence.

And evidence had been found. Cyrus Daly's laptop had been used to contact the cross-dresser who had been hired to kill Warren Blake, as well as others who billed themselves as contract killers on the dark web. There was also a record of internet searches concerning the jurors and the judge in the case. Most disturbing of all was the research Cyrus had performed on amusement park rides and their safety features, much of it went back years. It indicated that he had been behind the incident that killed Larry Huckel.

Tests were being performed on Cyrus's clothing. In the following days it would reveal the presence of blood, blood of a type that couldn't be his. Weeks later, DNA would prove that the blood belonged to the missing jury foreman.

For now, Cyrus Daly was officially just a wanted suspect, one the police and others in law enforcement desired badly.

CYRUS TURNED OFF HIS PHONE AND TOSSED IT IN A nearby trash can. He wasn't going to obtain his new identity a day too soon. And yet, he now needed to do more than change his name.

He turned and walked away from his apartment building. Six blocks later, he entered a barbershop. The place had four chairs. One of the barbers was free. He was a guy in his forties and must have been in charge, as he was telling the barber next to him that he needed him to work on Sunday. Cyrus climbed up into the elevated seat and heaved a sigh.

"I want you to shave off all my hair."

"All of it?" the barber asked.

"Yeah, um… I lost a bet."

The barber laughed and went to work.

Cyrus left the barbershop and felt the strange sensation of the breeze passing over his bare scalp. After making a stop at a drugstore, Cyrus went into a restaurant and entered their bathroom. It took him some time to do it, being unaccustomed as he was, but he managed to insert the set of brown-colored contact lenses he'd bought. Afterward, he put on a pair of non-prescription eyeglasses. With his shaved head and altered eye color, he saw a stranger looking back at him in the mirror.

The lenses made his eyes water, but he knew he'd get used to them. Cyrus waved at his reflection in the mirror, as he said goodbye to his old self.

STRIKE TWO

Nick Medina was already seated at the table inside the room where he was to speak to his client, Zander Hall. Hall was brought in, ordered to sit in a metal chair, then had his wrists shackled to the table. Medina took note of Hall's blackened right eye.

"Were you in a fight?"

"I was shoved by a guard. When I pushed him back another guard hit me in the face with a baton. I've spent the last week in solitary confinement."

"You look thinner. Are they feeding you?"

"I'm fed, but the food is shit."

"I have messages for you from our friend."

"Messages?"

"There are two. I found a new one as I was waiting to be led back here."

"I hope it's good news."

"I'll let you decide that," Medina said, then he gave Hall Cyrus's messages. The first one informed him that another juror had been killed and that Warren Blake was being targeted again. The second message was succinct. "I'm burned."

Medina saw Hall's shoulders slump as he received the news that the cops were on to Cyrus.

"Damn, I was hoping he would never get identified. At least he had a chance to get away."

"Does this mean there will be no more messages?"

"No, but he'll probably begin using the backup email account we set up. Start checking that. He might still make contact."

"All right. Is there anything else I can do for you?"

"Not unless you know a way to break out of here."

Medina looked around. The room they were in was near the center of the prison. He had to pass through a series of eight locked gates and countless guards and cameras to reach it while being escorted. Outside were two fences, a wall topped by razor wire, and guard towers. He couldn't imagine any way someone could escape.

"The laws change all the time, and then there are appeals... maybe someday you'll get free."

"Yeah, and maybe someday I'll be able to flap my arms and float into the air too. I'm fucked and we both know it. That's why I want Warren Blake dead. I don't want that bastard out there living his life while I'm stuck in here. I hired him to keep me free and he let me down. Now he's going to pay the price."

"If anything happens to Blake, they'll toss you back in the hole."

Hall smiled. "And I'll be laughing as they drag me into it."

TANNER WAS AT A SMALL AIRPORT IN PLAINVILLE, Connecticut, with Warren. They had been driven there in a bulletproof limousine that belonged to Joe Pullo. Tanner had asked for the favor the day before when he'd been in the city to visit Duke for supplies and weapons. He didn't want Warren out in the open any longer than was necessary. Keeping his father-in-law behind the deep-tinted, bullet-resistant windows of the limo seemed a good idea.

Their limo driver was a young man named Andre. Andre's nickname was Red, because he was of Russian descent. Red had saved Pullo's life and Joe had rewarded him by giving him an easy job with a fat salary. Red had most days off as Joe rarely used the limousine.

Once they'd arrived at the airport, Warren directed Red to the hangar his plane was housed in. He had called ahead and had the Cessna 172 readied for flight. The oil had been changed and the tanks topped off. All Warren needed to do was to give the plane a preflight inspection.

Warren used an app on his phone to open the hangar door. Red drove inside and parked near the plane. Tanner helped Red unload their gear as Warren began looking the plane over. When they had everything out of the trunk, Tanner handed Red a hundred dollars. Red had seemed more boy than man when Tanner first met him, the kid had matured and was more self-assured.

"Tell Joe I said thanks, Red."

"I will. Are you going to need me to pick you up too?"

"No. By the time we come back we should be able to rent a normal car."

"If you change your mind, I'll be here. And thanks for the tip."

Red left the hangar and headed back to Manhattan. After checking a rear door to see if it was locked, Tanner moved to a window with a pair of binoculars.

"What are you looking for?" Warren said.

"Signs of a sniper."

"I'm sorry I asked," Warren said.

THERE WERE NO SNIPERS. HOWEVER, THERE WAS A killer about. He went by the single name of Otto and had been contacted by Cyrus on the dark web. Otto considered himself to be a pro and was eager to earn his fee. He had no love for lawyers, not even defense attorneys.

Otto had done research on Blake and saw an article where he mentioned that he was a pilot. After paying a hacker he learned which airport Warren Blake frequented and discovered that Blake had his own plane. Otto had been staking out the hangar since early in the morning. He had assumed that Blake would be on the run after it became known that another juror had died. It only made sense for the man to fly off in his own plane rather than risk exposing himself to the crowds of strangers inside an airport. If he'd been wrong, he would have looked for another opportunity to kill Warren Blake. The last place he would visit was the man's home. If Blake had hunkered down inside his house, he wouldn't be alone. Otto had no intention of walking into a trap set by a prepared group of armed security guards, or worse, the police.

He was dressed like a mechanic in a pair of baggy secondhand coveralls and a denim cap. To add authenticity, he had an oily rag hanging out of his back pocket.

When the limo parked in front of Blake's hangar Otto had whispered, "Yes," to himself. He was proud that he had been right in anticipating the lawyer's next move. The car drove inside the hangar and Otto moved closer by approaching it from the rear. He had to find out if Blake had arrived with bodyguards, and if so, how many. Whoever they were, they would die along with the lawyer. Otto had a Remington 1100 shotgun hidden under his coveralls. It had a twelve-inch barrel and a pistol grip. Once he was inside the hangar, he would open up on anything that moved.

Otto paused at the side of a small utility shed and sent a quick text to the client.

Target in sight. Caught him trying to fly away.

THEY HAD LOWERED THE HANGAR DOOR AFTER RED'S departure even though they were leaving within minutes. No one could view the plane until they were on the field. Warren would be vulnerable until he had them in the air. The surrounding terrain was a series of small hills where a sniper could hide among trees. If such a person was out there, he or she would have to be an exceptional shot. The nearest hills were over half a mile away.

Tanner was glassing the hills with the binoculars for a second time when the faint sound reached his ears. It was the sound of a pen falling. After checking the rear door to make sure it was locked, Tanner had left a pen balanced on its handle. Had the pen fallen on its own or had someone tried the doorknob?

Tanner moved toward the door while signaling Warren to stay inside the plane.

Warren mouthed the words, "What is it?" as Tanner went past him. Tanner didn't answer; he was preoccupied with listening for more sounds while sneaking looks back at the man-size entrance that was beside the hangar door. It was possible the guy at the rear could be a diversion while someone entered at the front.

As he grew closer to the door while approaching it at an angle, Tanner heard what sounded like scratching. Someone was picking the lock. They were not expert at it and were having trouble. There was a rack of tools near the door. Tanner claimed a large wrench and held it in his left hand as he pressed himself against the wall beside the door.

When he saw the small indicator on the

doorknob rotate from a vertical position to a horizontal one, Tanner knew the lock had been defeated. As the handle on the door twisted, Tanner raised the wrench.

Yes! Otto thought as he felt the lock disengage. He stuffed the pick he had been using back into a pocket and removed the shotgun from hiding. With his right hand gripping the weapon he turned the doorknob slowly with his left.

He eased the door open. It was made of metal and he feared that it might squeak and let it be known that he was there. He wanted to announce his presence by ripping Blake's chest apart with buckshot.

With the door opened two inches he could see the plane in the middle of the hangar. If Blake wasn't alone, he and his guests weren't talking. Otto smiled. One kill would be ideal. He was only being paid to murder Warren Blake. Any bodyguards or family members caught in the line of fire would be extra work. Otto didn't like working for free.

Emboldened by the silence, he pushed the door open further and eased his head in to get a better look. Otto was only able to register movement from his left before pain exploded in his head. It was followed by darkness.

W<small>ARREN CLIMBED FROM THE PLANE AND RUSHED OVER</small> to look at Otto after Tanner dragged the man's body inside the hangar.

"Is he dead?"

"Not yet; I want to talk to him first." Tanner claimed the shotgun and gave it a nod of approval. He would add it to the arsenal he was bringing along on the trip.

"You plan to kill him, Cody?"

"Yes."

"Why not hand him over to the police and let them interrogate him?"

"They'll charge him with breaking and entering and maybe slap a weapons charge on him. Then he'll be back on the streets and will likely kill someone else someday."

"But he was here to kill me; we know that?"

Tanner smiled at his father-in-law. "How would you spin this if you were his lawyer?"

Warren moaned as he realized Tanner was right. They had no proof that the man was there to commit murder. Depending on his record, Warren would have had him released on bail the next day.

"I can't believe I'm asking this, but how do you plan to kill him?"

Tanner grabbed Otto under his arms. "Help me get him on the plane."

OTTO WAS STRAPPED INTO A SEAT ON THE AIRPLANE. He awoke to the worse pain he'd ever felt in his life. He wasn't a drinker and had no experience with hangovers, but he imagined that the agony in his skull must be what they were like. Opening his eyes brought more pain as sunlight caused him to squint. There was also a loud rumbling sound that made everything worse.

"Whatever that noise is, can someone shut it off. It's too loud."

"That's the sound of the plane's engine," Tanner told him. "If Warren shuts it off, we all die."

"Plane? I'm on a plane?"

"For now. Who hired you to kill Warren?"

Otto tried to focus his eyes on Tanner. "Who are you?"

"I'm the one asking questions. What's your name?"

"Otto."

"Who hired you?"

"I want a lawyer."

"Warren, would you like to represent this man?"

"Hell no."

"You're out of luck; he's the only lawyer on the plane. Tell me who hired you or I'll give you an ache in your knee that will make the one in your head feel like pleasure."

"I was hired over the internet. The money came in the mail. I can't help you."

"I assumed that, but I had to ask." Tanner held up Otto's phone. Otto had neglected to delete the last text he'd sent off to Cyrus.

"This was sent to your employer?"

"Yeah, but I doubt you can trace it."

"So do I. Is there anything else you can tell us?"

"This wasn't personal, you know? I'm just a guy doing a job."

"Believe me, I understand."

Otto sighed. "Good. Where are we headed. I see water down there."

"We're several miles off the coast of Massachusetts."

"Out at sea? In this little plane?"

"It's a detour."

"To where?"

Tanner pointed out a window. "Look over there."

When Otto turned his head, Tanner hit him with

the wrench, harder than the last blow, but not enough to crack his skull. It rendered him unconscious again. Any blood the blow released would be absorbed by Otto's hair and the cap he was wearing. A hand was placed over Otto's mouth and nose. With the state he was in, he never struggled. In a matter of minutes, he died from lack of oxygen.

"Good Lord," Warren whispered.

"How's it look on your end?" Tanner asked him.

"We're clear. Check out the back."

Tanner saw nothing but blue sky surrounding them and the white dots of pleasure craft many miles away. The plane was flying low and slow. Tanner climbed into the front passenger seat and opened the door as Warren flew the plane lower. Wind resistance kept the door from opening fully.

Tanner unbuckled Otto and hustled him up front. Between Otto's dead weight and the pressure of Tanner's foot, the door opened enough so that the body tumbled out. The corpse entered the sea and disappeared beneath the water. It was followed by the wrench.

Tanner closed and locked the door, then strapped himself in.

"That was... I... I don't know what to call it," Warren said.

"Necessary. It was necessary."

"If I had been making this trip alone as I'd

planned, I'd be dead already. Thank you for saving my life, Cody."

"You're welcome. I hope he's the last one."

"We should be safe once we're at the cabin."

"Right," Tanner said, but he wasn't certain that more killers wouldn't come along.

13

LUCKY

SARA WAS STAYING AT THE PENTHOUSE WHILE HER father and Tanner headed to Maine. Accompanying her and Lucas was Warren's live-in housekeeper, Mrs. Johnson. Lydia Johnson was suitably impressed by the level of luxury the penthouse afforded.

"This is so lovely, Sara."

"Thank you. We love life on the ranch but it's always a pleasure to come back to the city."

"Do you think we'll have to stay here for long?"

"I hope not. Jake and I are both doing what we can to find the man who hired the killer to attack Daddy in his office. Before coming here there was a break in the case that should lead to something."

"I'm worried about your father. I pray that he stays safe in Maine."

"He's with Cody. My husband is resourceful."

Sara helped Mrs. Johnson to settle into a guest room. After placing Lucas in a playpen that sat in a corner of the kitchen, she poured water to use in making a pot of coffee.

Mrs. Johnson entered the room and shooed her away. "Let me do that."

"Nope. You sit and relax. When you're here, you're my guest."

"All right, but I'm not accustomed to sitting still."

"I hope you know how much Jenny and I appreciate everything you do for Daddy, Mrs. Johnson. If he were alone in that house and fending for himself, he might be eating frozen dinners every night."

"I enjoy having someone to cook and care for, although your father isn't home nights very often these days."

"You mean he's spending time with Nina?"

"Yes."

"What do you think of her?"

"She seems lovely," Mrs. Johnson said, but it was voiced in a flat tone.

Sara smiled. "You don't like her either, do you?"

Mrs. Johnson put her cup down. "I didn't say that. I've had very little interaction with the woman. I do think she's a little young for your father."

"Is that a polite way of saying she's a gold digger?"

"Now, Sara, don't put words in my mouth."

"I don't mean to. There's something about Nina Girardin that doesn't sit right with me. What do you know about her?"

"She's been married before. That man was also older than her."

"How much older?"

"She was thirty-eight and her husband was fifty when they married. He died only a year later of a heart attack."

"She told you this?"

"I overheard her and Warren talking," Mrs. Johnson said, she then shrugged slightly. "I was moving about, doing my chores, you tend to hear things. I wasn't being a snoop."

"I believe you."

"It seems the husband left her money. Miss Girardin used it to open her first boutique."

"Yes, Daddy said she was in business."

Mrs. Johnson waved a hand. "That's enough about your father's lady friend. I don't like to gossip."

"I just wanted to learn more about Nina."

Mrs. Johnson took her cup to the sink and cleaned it. "Call me if you need me, Sara. I'll be in my room unpacking. Afterward, I think I'll go out and explore the city some. It's been years since I've been here."

"Okay, Mrs. Johnson."

Sara thought over what she had learned about Nina, including the dead husband. It only made her uneasiness about Nina deepen. She took out her phone and sent a text off to Kate Barlow.

Let me know what you can find out about a woman named Nina Girardin.

THE FLIGHT TO THE CABIN PASSED IN A SOMBER MOOD after disposing of Otto's body. When they stopped to refuel in Bangor, where they also ate lunch, Warren's disposition brightened, and he began asking Tanner about his flying experience. He was surprised to learn that Tanner had a license to fly helicopters.

"You've really taken to aviation in a big way."

"It was long overdue. Spenser had become a pilot at a much earlier age."

"You look up to him, and I can see why. I found him to be interesting when we spoke at your wedding."

"He's been like a father to me. If not for him I would have died along with my family."

Their remaining time in the air passed well as they talked, and soon, they were at their destination. That was when they saw they had a problem.

"Damn it. There's a downed tree lying across the

runway. It's not leaving nearly enough room for me to land."

"We passed a field south of here. You might be able to land her there."

Warren banked the plane. "I know the area. Let's go have a look."

The field was flat overall, and the wild grass had yet to rise high in the early days of spring.

"I don't see any tree stumps," Tanner said. "But there's a spot on the north end that looks like it might have been on fire recently."

"There was an incident. I'll tell you about it later."

"Why is this one area cleared of trees?"

"About six years ago a group of land developers bought this acreage with plans to create a lake between two streams. Once that was completed, they were going to build luxury vacation homes and sell them. They cut a path through the trees between here and the nearest road with the intention of using this patch of land as a staging area. They ran out of money when a major backer abandoned the project. That field down there had been cleared of tree stumps. That doesn't mean we're not in for a bumpy landing."

"Will you be able to walk to the cabin from here? It's about four miles."

"I can do it. I'm on the treadmill every morning. A four-mile hike shouldn't kill me."

"Eight miles. We'll have to walk back and retrieve the plane once the runway is cleared."

"I'll make it. Anyway, we can rest a while between trips."

"Not for very long, or it will get dark."

Warren circled around, made his approach, then pulled up at the last second.

"I want to try coming in from a different angle, that way we'll be going up a slight incline as we brake to a stop."

Tanner agreed it was the right play. As they climbed again, Tanner saw movement below, where there was a small gap between trees. It was a dark shape moving fast. It looked too small to be a man. He assumed it was an animal of some kind. Before he could identify what it was, they were past it. When Warren brought them down again, he landed well and maintained control of the plane despite the bumpy ground. They came to a stop fifty yards away from the surrounding trees.

"Good job, Warren."

"Thanks. We should have enough light left to remove that fallen tree and move the plane to the landing strip."

"Are there tools? I'll need an axe."

"I can do better than that. Bill had a fully stocked shed. There's a chainsaw. The only problem is that the gas might have gone bad. I haven't been up here since last August."

A dog barked from the edge of the trees to the left of the plane. Tanner realized it was the animal he had seen from the air. From a distance he looked like a black Labrador.

"I wonder where that dog came from," Warren said.

Sunlight glinted off a collar around the hound's neck. "I'm going over to him," Tanner said. "It looks like he has tags."

"I'll come with you."

"No, stay here, and keep the engine running. If there's trouble, take off."

"I won't just leave you here, Cody."

"I can take care of myself if I know you're safe."

"This can't be trouble. No one knows we're here except for the family, and Nina."

"It's probably just a lost dog. I'll be right back."

The dog's tail wagged as Tanner grew nearer to it. Up close, Tanner could see that the dog was panting.

"What happened, fella?"

Tanner moved his hand toward the collar carefully, in case the dog tried to bite him. The dog allowed him to handle the tags as he continued to pant. It appeared the lab had run some distance to reach them.

"Lucky," Tanner said, as he read the name on the dog tags. There was also a phone number to call.

"C'mon boy, follow me back to the plane. I'll try to get in touch with your people once we're settled in at the cabin. We'll see about getting you some food too."

The dog wagged his tail and followed along at Tanner's side. Seeing him coming back, Warren powered down the plane and joined them.

"He's a beauty."

"He is. The collar says his name is Lucky. I think he must have gotten separated from his owner. There's a number on his collar I'll call later."

Tanner had stored his things in a backpack. He removed a few items, including a satellite phone, and claimed the shotgun that had belonged to Otto. Along with the five shells it held, Otto had been carrying five more in his pocket.

As he checked his cell phone, Tanner saw he had a signal. That surprised him, as Warren had stated that there was no service in the area. Warren saw him looking at his phone and explained.

"There's no service at the cabin. I usually get a signal if I walk a few miles south or east of it. Someday they'll boost the signal or put up another tower and I won't need to pack a satellite phone when I come here."

"Satellite phones are always handy anyway," Tanner said, as they began their trek.

It was early April and the trees had yet to bloom but did have buds on them. The temperature was comfortable, and the humidity was low.

Part of the walk took them up a steep hill. Warren looked winded when they reached the top but recovered his breath quickly. The dog stayed by Tanner's side for the most part, only leaving him to dart after a squirrel that scampered up a tree to get away. Lucky came close to catching the tree rat.

The cabin looked newer than Tanner had expected it to be. Warren remarked that he'd had some work done on it in recent years.

"That bay window is new, and I added a larger propane tank and backed it up with a few solar panels. I also replaced the septic system when I first took possession of the cabin."

"I spotted the solar panels from the air, but I don't remember seeing a propane tank."

"It's underground and has a thousand-gallon capacity. It should be about half full. There's also a wood burning stove and two fireplaces."

"You mentioned yesterday that there was a pickup truck. The gas in it must be old too."

"No, it will be fine. I have someone looking after the place. He also makes sure the truck stays in running condition. I let him use it when I'm not here. When I spoke to him yesterday, he said that he last drove it three weeks ago to buy lumber and returned it with a full tank."

"Good. We'll drive into town tomorrow to stock up on food."

The interior of the cabin was about a thousand square feet. Most of the space was on the lower level, with the bedroom in the loft area. At the rear was a small deck.

Warren unlocked the tool shed where the chainsaw was kept. Tanner had trouble getting it started but once it was running it made fast work of the fallen tree. As he cut it into pieces, Warren moved the sections off the runway. Many of them rolled well, making the work easier.

They went back inside the cabin and Warren turned on the valves that would allow water to flow from the well, while he was doing that, Tanner inspected the doors and windows, then fed the dog a can of corned beef hash he'd found in a cupboard. Lucky the dog wolfed down the food then sniffed his way around the living room and tiny kitchen area.

When he was through gathering scents, Lucky plopped in front of the dormant fireplace. Warren flipped the master circuit breaker on, and the sound of a generator rumbled to life from outside. It was in its own small shed that was insulated to lessen the noise. Once the generator hit its stride the rumble became a low growl.

Since they had the time and Warren wanted to rest a bit before hiking back to the plane, Tanner decided to call the number on Lucky's collar. The area code placed it as being in Syracuse, New York. After five rings, an elderly female voice answered.

"Hello?"

Tanner explained why he was calling and heard the woman gasp. "You have Lucky?"

"Yes, ma'am. I'm at a remote area in northern Maine."

"Maine? Did you say Maine?"

"Yes."

"Where exactly?"

Tanner mentioned the name of the nearest town.

"Sweet Lord," the old lady said, and Tanner heard the stress in her voice. There was another note present; it sounded like wonder.

"Why is that news upsetting to you?"

After a pause, the old woman spoke again. "Sir, my son was a pilot. He took his wife and two boys on a trip to Canada… along the way, the plane was struck by lightning… they all died when it crashed in a field." The old woman had trouble getting the last part out.

"I'm sorry for your loss. I know what it's like to lose loved ones."

"Lucky was here when the crash occurred. My husband was still alive then but died of a stroke a few weeks later. I think it was losing our son and his grandbabies that killed him. Lucky was to stay with us until our son returned. The dog took off that night and the next day we heard about the tragedy. It sounds as if Lucky made his way to where my family... to where they were."

"I've heard similar stories about animals," Tanner said, as he stared at the dog.

"I still have family around, my two daughters, thank God, but none of us can care for the dog. I know you're a stranger and that it's not your problem, but can you please find a good home for Lucky? My grandson Bobby loved that dog so much."

"Don't worry. I'll see that he's cared for."

"Thank you."

"How old is the dog?"

"Lucky was just a puppy when Bobby got him. That was almost two years ago."

When the call ended, Tanner explained to Warren what he had learned about the dog.

"That burnt area. That's where the plane crashed, isn't it?"

Warren nodded. "It was a tragedy. Howard, the man who runs the general store in town, he's the one who stops by here now and then to check on the cabin for me. He called me at the time and told me what had happened. I didn't want to bring it up while we were attempting to land in practically the same spot."

"That dog made it here somehow from New York State."

"Incredible."

"I'll have to find a home for him. If not here, then we'll fly him back to Connecticut with us and look for someone to take him."

"He's well-named. If we hadn't shown up today, he might have been on his own in these woods for the rest of his life. Lucky for him we're here."

"Lucky for us too. He'll react to strange sounds long before we'll hear them. Dogs are a good early warning system."

"They're good judges of character as well, and it looks like he's taken a liking to you." Warren studied the lab. "He's a little underweight, but he must have been hunting down prey while he made his way here from New York."

"Add dog food to the shopping list."

Warren stood and stretched. "Let's go get the plane."

They locked up the cabin and began the trek back to the field. As Lucky walked along beside Tanner, his tail wagged in contentment.

14

TRY, TRY, AGAIN

SEVERAL DAYS LATER, THE JAPANESE ASSASSIN, TARAN, picked the locks on Warren Blake's front door quicker than some might unlock them if they had a key. After relocking the door behind him, he checked the alarm pad and was pleased to see that it had failed to notice his invasion.

Had it done so, the alarm would sound off after sixty seconds if the right four-digit code wasn't entered. Once that happened, staff at the alarm company's monitoring center would place a call to the house. If the call went unanswered or if someone responding failed to reply correctly to a security question, police would be alerted and sent to the residence.

Taran had avoided that by activating a hand-held two-way radio. The two-way could be made to transmit at a frequency of 433 megahertz. Warren Blake's alarm system worked at the same frequency. A sensor was secured to the door by adhesive and its complementing magnet was stuck to the door frame. If the two pieces were to separate while the alarm system was armed, the sensor would transmit a signal to the system's base station or alarm pad. That signal also worked on a frequency of 433 megahertz.

When Taran activated the two-way radio, it sent out a signal at a strength of five watts. Warren's alarm sensor's signal strength was barely a few milliwatts. With the two-way transmitting on its frequency, the sensor's weak signal was drowned out and never communicated with the alarm system's base station. In fact, the superior strength of the two-way radio's signal had likely disabled similar alarm systems owned by Warren's neighbors. It was a serious flaw in the security system's design that Taran took advantage of to break into Blake's home.

There were no motion detectors as he'd expected there to be. Their absence was usually explained by the homeowner having pets, but Taran saw none about. As he assumed it would be, the house was unoccupied. Perhaps the human residents of the home had taken their pets with them. That was fine. He had come there seeking information on Blake and wanted to avoid having to deal with anyone.

In the kitchen, Taran sat a small device on top of

a corner of the refrigerator. It was a combination camera/motion detector. More of the inconspicuous devices were placed about the home with one being left near the front door. If anyone entered the house Taran would be alerted by his phone, which would vibrate.

A careful search of Blake's personal papers revealed that the lawyer was a pilot. A photo of a smiling Blake standing beside his aircraft was hanging on the wall. Taran memorized the registration number that was painted on the plane's tail. He could use that to track Blake if he had flown away.

Another photo on the wall stunned Taran when he saw it. It was a family photo taken in recent years that showed Blake with his youngest daughter and another man. That other man was Tanner.

Taran had viewed a photo of Tanner once. It had been a mugshot taken by Mexican authorities. That photo had been erased from all official databases in the intervening years. Taran had also seen the assassin in the flesh recently in New York City, although at the time, Tanner had been wearing sunglasses. There was no mistaking those eyes. The man in the picture with Blake was Tanner.

Taran took the photo from the wall, carefully removed it from its frame, then checked the rear of it. There were words written in Blake's handwriting.

Me, Sara, and Cody at the ranch.

The words were accompanied by a date from the previous year.

"Cody?" Taran whispered. Tanner's real name was Cody. He went in search of other photos of Tanner and found them. One such photo showed Tanner with Sara and Lucas.

He's married and a father, Taran thought.

Taran came across a file containing receipts for veterinarian services concerning a cat. The paperwork went back many years; however, the cat had died recently. That explained the lack of motion detectors in the home. Further searching through documents revealed that Blake owned a cabin in the state of Maine. The lawyer also possessed several rental properties nearby in his home state of Connecticut. One of those rentals was currently unoccupied as paperwork revealed that a tenant had recently moved out. Taran copied the addresses and put everything back as he had found it.

His phone vibrated in his pocket at the same moment he heard the front door opening. That was followed by the sound of someone entering the code into the keypad that would disable the alarm.

Taran checked his phone and saw that a woman had come into the house. As she moved through the rooms, each of Taran's devices activated and sent video of her to his phone. It appeared she was headed straight to the kitchen. Taran recognized her. He had seen her in some of the photos on the wall.

After entering the kitchen, the woman went to a counter and grabbed a ceramic bowl. The word *SUGAR* was written on it in a fancy script. She reached into a cabinet and took down a mixing bowl to dump the sugar into it. Afterward, she took something from her purse. It was a clear plastic bag. The substance inside it was white. The woman mixed the contents from the baggie with the sugar, then poured the sugar back into its ceramic bowl. Before leaving the house, she washed the mixing bowl and the metal whisk she had used, dried them, and put them back from where she had taken them.

She paused at the threshold and glanced backwards over her shoulder, staring at the sugar bowl. Taran wondered for a moment if she had regretted what she had just done. If so, it was a fleeting emotion. The woman moved through the home and out the front door, enabling the alarm before she left.

If Taran hadn't seen her image among Blake's photos he would have thought she was a fellow assassin out to fulfill the contract on Warren Blake. Her actions were an obvious attempt to poison the man. If anyone else used the sugar, they would die as well.

Taran spent several more minutes in the home

before once again disabling the alarm system. He then went in search of Warren Blake.

Cyrus had stayed the last few days in a tourist trap of a hotel. He'd checked in carrying a new suitcase that held new clothes. Except for what he'd been wearing, everything was back at his apartment. He sure as hell was never going there, not with the FBI ready to pounce on him.

Not wanting to stay anywhere for too long, he checked out and moved to a different hotel. He didn't own a car and rented them infrequently as he was lousy at driving. He'd had three fender benders by the time he was nineteen and decided that driving just wasn't for him. Living in New York City, he'd had other options for transportation, so rarely needed to climb behind the wheel.

He'd felt cooped up in his new hotel room and went out on the streets to move around. He was getting used to the brown contact lenses sooner than he would have thought, but he was startled every time he passed a mirror and saw his shaved head.

It had been days since the assassin named Otto had reported that he was about to kill Warren Blake. There was no news of Blake being found dead, while Otto had failed to report on what had happened.

If the assassin had botched an attempt to kill Warren Blake and been arrested it would have made the news. Cyrus was sure that meant that something had gone very wrong.

He should have gotten rid of the phone he was using to communicate with Otto. He'd held onto it a little longer, as he was still hopeful of hearing from Otto. He paused as he was about to cross a street and powered the phone on to give it one last check for messages before tossing it into the gutter. There were no new messages, but the phone rang. Cyrus was pleased to see that it was Otto calling—or so he thought.

"Hello?"

Tanner's voice came over the phone. "Cyrus Daly. Your man Otto is dead. Anyone you send after Warren Blake will die."

"What? I... who is this?"

"I'm Blake's bodyguard. If you send anyone else after him, I'll not only kill them, but I'll come looking for you too."

Cyrus bristled at being threatened. He knew he didn't appear menacing, but he was a nasty piece of work who had killed dozens in his lifetime.

"You don't scare me. As for Blake, he's dead. I'll just keep sending killers after him until the job gets done."

"Or you'll be caught and placed in a cell next to your friend, Hall."

"Wrong. The police won't catch me, and neither will you. If you want to live stay away from Warren Blake. I promised Hall that I'd have Blake killed and that's what's going to happen."

"Let it go, Daly. You don't owe Hall anything."

"Blake is a dead man," Cyrus said. He had begun shouting and noticed that several people walking by were giving him odd looks. Cyrus ended the call, walked to the curb, and dropped the phone down a sewer grate. It made a splashing sound as it struck water.

IN MAINE, TANNER LOOKED AT THE CELL PHONE IN his hand. He'd been playing a long shot by calling Cyrus's number and was surprised when it was answered.

The bad news was that Cyrus was determined to have Warren killed. The good news is that anyone he hired would have a difficult time finding them. Difficult, but as he well knew from experience, it was not impossible. If Daly wasn't captured soon, Tanner decided he would suggest to Warren that they move to another location. It would make it infinitely more difficult for an assassin to find them.

He was outside a general store and leaning against the pickup truck they were using. It was an old red Ford F-150 with rusty metal bumpers. In town, Tanner could get a cell signal. The shop had a wide window that allowed him to keep Warren in sight.

He had used the satellite phone while they were still at the cabin that morning to speak to Sara. He missed her. Tanner wished he could be in Manhattan with Sara and Lucas, but his priority was to keep Warren safe.

Lucky was seated beside Tanner outside the store. The dog had a habit of staying close to him. They were in town to buy more food and Tanner thought he'd found a home for Lucky when a girl of ten was fawning over the Lab.

Tanner let it be known that Lucky was available for adoption, but the girl's mother said no.

"We'll get you a smaller dog. Something that can fit on your lap."

The girl pouted but didn't argue and Lucky seemed content to stay with Tanner.

Tanner was happy to have him around as well. He'd placed motion detectors and wired up a few cameras, but as he'd told Warren the day they'd come across the Lab, dogs were good early warning systems. It had been mild over the last few nights, so Tanner piled spare blankets on the porch as a bed for

Lucky. There had been some rope in the tool shed. Tanner placed Lucky on a twenty-foot lead so he could wander off the porch to pee. If anyone approached the cabin after making it past the motion detectors, the dog would have sounded the alarm by barking.

Each morning, Tanner freed Lucky from the rope and was rewarded by having his hand licked. Breakfast for Lucky had been another can of hash. Once they had visited town, Tanner bought the hound proper food for a canine and threw in a chew toy.

Warren came out of the store talking on a cell phone. He was speaking to Nina. When he was saying goodbye, he told Nina he loved her.

"How's Nina doing?"

Warren smiled. "She says she misses me too. No offense, but I wish she had joined me on this trip instead of you."

"Otto might have given her more trouble than he did me."

"Good point," Warren said, as Tanner opened the door on the truck.

INSIDE THE GENERAL STORE, A YOUNG CLERK CALLED to his boss. "I'm going out back for a smoke break."

"Don't be long," his boss yelled back.

The youth, Alex Finkle, had stringy hair and a thin build. He dreamed of being a rock star someday and was saving up money to move to Los Angeles. The call he was about to make was intended to ensure that he'd soon have a good chunk of change to add to his savings.

A deep voice answered. "Young Mr. Finkle, does this call mean what I hope it means?"

"Yeah, man. That old guy Blake is here. He's staying at his cabin, the one I sent you directions to."

"Excellent."

"You're going to pay me, right? Five hundred bucks."

"That was our deal."

"Cool."

"Yes," the deep voice said. "Very cool." The kid would never see a dime of that money.

AFTER THEY HAD RETURNED TO THE CABIN AND HAD coffee, Warren sat on an old leather couch looking through a box of fishing lures. In the two days they'd been at the cabin Warren had only sat around and read. Tired of being cooped up, he decided to try his luck with rod and reel.

"Do you fish, Cody?"

"I do it now and then. I prefer deep sea fishing."

Warren grinned. "So do I. I once caught a Yellowfin tuna in Florida. The thing weighed more than I did." Warren laughed. "Sara and Jenny were still at home then. We ate so much tuna that month they got sick of it." He smiled. "That was a good trip."

"The next time you're in Texas we'll head down to the Gulf. Romeo has a boat and is an expert fisherman."

"That would be nice."

Tanner told Warren about his conversation with Cyrus.

"It sounds as if he'll be recruiting more killers."

"Yes, but there's a good chance that the police or FBI will capture Cyrus now that they know who he is. I also have people looking for him."

"And what if they don't find him? I can't hide from paid killers for the rest of my life."

"You won't have to; I'll see to that."

"How?"

"I'll have to go after Cyrus myself. Unlike the police I don't have other things dividing my attention. I can also get help from Spenser and Romeo if needed. Between the three of us, we'll track down Cyrus."

Warren tossed a lure back into the box with disgust. "What a mess this has turned into. Damn Zander Hall. That bastard kills his wife and when he's found guilty all he can think to do is blame me for his incarceration. I've been threatened by clients before, but this is insane."

"It will end, Warren. You won't have to hide forever."

"If Hall was here right now, I'd throttle him."

Tanner didn't want to say so, but he had already realized that Hall's death would be the only way to ensure Warren's safety in the long run, no matter what became of Cyrus Daly. Hall was in prison. He'd have opportunities to offer a contract to fellow inmates who would be released after serving their sentences or were paroled. As long as Zander Hall lived, Warren's life was at risk. Hall had to die; the trick would be getting to him behind bars. Tanner had been thinking about how best to do that.

CYRUS USED A NEW LAPTOP TO MAKE CONTACT WITH A team of assassins. This group wanted a hundred and fifty thousand dollars to kill Warren Blake. Cyrus gladly paid it from the funds Hall had left him. The kill squad consisted of a team of four. They boasted of a perfect success rate and specialized in difficult targets.

He had always been one to plan ahead. When Hall let him know that he wanted Blake dead if found guilty, Cyrus had gone to work lining up assassins. As someone who had been killing throughout his life for pleasure, it amazed him how much murder for hire could be worth.

There was, as in most professions, a wide range of skill sets and acumen. At the top was a mythic figure named Tanner. He was rumored to cost millions and was the latest in a long line of killers. When Cyrus came across an episode of the television series *Blue Truth Investigates*, he abandoned his efforts to find a way to contact Tanner. The show had compelling evidence to suggest that Tanner was nothing more than a myth.

Cyrus had contacted and made deals with several assassins. Some, such as the group he was engaging now, had received a non-refundable down payment to remain on standby. Cyrus hadn't thought it would take more than one try to kill Blake, but he was a thorough man who liked to be prepared.

In all, he had made contact with four different levels of assassins. The kill squad were mid-range, next up was a Russian assassin who normally operated in Russia and Europe. Cyrus hoped he didn't have to call on the man's services. His price was steep; nearly half a million in US currency.

There was another killer Cyrus had contacted through an intermediary. If he were forced to use him and meet his price, he would have to spend the majority of the funds Hall had left him. He'd sent details to the man about the target along with an inquiry stating he was willing to offer a down payment in case he was needed. He had heard nothing back from the assassin and assumed he wasn't interested. Still, the man was an option if needed. He was said to possibly be the best assassin in the world. He went by the name Taran.

THE LEADER OF THE KILL TEAM SENT A TEXT SAYING that they were ready to proceed as soon as payment was received. Cyrus sent more money to the foreign bank account he had previously directed the deposit to and waited for a reply that it had been received.

The message came swiftly. They had received the money and would engage the target within thirty-six hours.

Cyrus stared at the screen in confusion. Warren Blake had flown off in his plane to God only knew where. How could they kill him in such a short window of time? It would be impressive if they could locate him in a week.

Cyrus informed them that Blake was in hiding and wasn't at his home in Connecticut. A phone number appeared on the screen, along with instructions to call.

Cyrus removed the new phone he'd bought and dialed the number. It was answered on the first ring by a deep male voice.

"Hello. If the news reports are correct, I'm speaking to Cyrus Daly, yes?"

"That's right. I guess I won't bother to ask your name."

"I wouldn't give it."

"How do you expect to find Blake in a matter of hours?"

"We don't. It took us days. We began gathering info on the target when you first approached us and made provisions to locate him if and when it became necessary. Earlier today we received a call from one of the contacts we'd made online. We know exactly where to find Warren Blake. He's at a cabin in northern Maine"

"That's damn good work."

"We're pros, Mr. Daly, unlike that clown in the dress you hired instead of us."

"I was trying to save money, and who knew a damn lawyer would be so hard to kill?"

"He must have protection."

"That's right, a bodyguard. The ballsy bastard called me and told me to back down or he'd kill me. He's already killed the second guy I sent after Blake."

"You're saying there's one man guarding Blake?"

"Yes."

"He'll be handled as part of the contract; we've never failed, and we won't this time."

Cyrus smiled into the phone. "I'm glad we talked. You inspire confidence."

"You get what you pay for in this life, Mr. Daly."

"I hope that's true."

"I'll call you by noon two days from now."

"What if I don't hear from you by then?"

The deep voice chuckled. "You'll hear from us. Blake's bodyguard is no match for my team. Goodbye, Mr. Daly."

The call ended. Cyrus placed his phone on the desk in his hotel room and signed off the computer. If the man with the deep voice killed Blake it would leave him free to travel and begin his new life.

Cyrus laid down on the bed and closed his eyes. Soon, he would have good news to send to Hall. He fell asleep within seconds, confident that Warren Blake would die.

15

A PRETTY FACE, AN EVIL MIND

In Manhattan, Adamo Conti entered a barbershop as he made his rounds collecting for the Giacconi Family. The protection payments were to protect those paying from the Giacconis themselves. It was well known that you either paid or your business might suffer a tragic fire some night. Despite that, the payments bought you real protection as well. The Giacconis weren't the only ones who knew how to start a blaze.

Twenty-two years earlier, the granddaughter of the barbershop's owner had been raped and brutalized while away at college in another state. A police investigation uncovered the culprit and he was identified by the granddaughter and four other women he had raped.

Sam Giacconi had been running things back

then. That week, he himself paid a visit to the barbershop with a young man in tow. When the owner, the rape victim's grandfather handed him the weekly envelope with a shaking hand, Giacconi waved it off.

"I'm not here to take; I'm here to give." Sam Giacconi handed the man a photo of the sexual predator who had raped his granddaughter. In the photo, the man was lying in a pool of his own blood, having had his genitals cut off with a knife inside his cell. Giacconi stabbed a finger at the photo. "That piece of crap will never hurt your granddaughter again. He was locked in a cell a thousand miles from here and we still got to him for hurting one of our own, your granddaughter."

The barber had thanked him profusely. Giacconi had nodded while saying it was his pleasure to deal justice to such an animal as the rapist. He left the barbershop as the young man accompanying him held the door open. That young man had been Joe Pullo.

CONTI ACCEPTED THE ENVELOPE WHILE ASKING IF there had been any problems. The current owner of the barbershop, the rape victim's brother, said that everything was fine. Conti turned to leave then remembered that he had another question to ask. He took out a photo of Cyrus Daly and showed it to the barber. "Have you seen this guy?"

The man squinted at the photo, rubbed his chin, then nodded. "That's the guy who lost the bet."

"What do you mean?"

"He came in here to get his hair shaved off because he lost a bet. At least, that's what he said."

"Has he been back?"

"No."

"Take down a number. If you see him, I want you to call."

"I will."

Sara opened the door to the penthouse to let Kate Barlow in. Kate had information about Nina Girardin. Mrs. Johnson was out doing the shopping, as she insisted on contributing in some manner while staying with Sara.

There was a silver carafe and a set of cups on the coffee table in the living room. Sara asked Kate if she wanted coffee and was told no. Before sitting, Kate walked over to the playpen and gazed down at Lucas, who was asleep.

"They are so precious at that age," Kate said. The remark caused Sara to ask a question.

"Do you and Michael have children?"

The corners of Kate's lips turned downward. "We have a son and a daughter. They don't talk to us."

"I'm sorry. That must be difficult for you."

"It's for the best," Kate said, as she turned from the playpen and took a seat. "I'll tell you what we found out about Nina Girardin and then leave you in peace."

"There's no need to rush. And are you certain you don't want coffee?"

Kate stared at Sara. "Why are you being nice? I know you don't like me."

"I didn't like you or trust you because of what you did to the graves of Cody's family."

"I can't tell you how much we regret doing that, and I don't just mean because it made us targets of your husband. I'll apologize again even though I know that doesn't change anything."

"Cody has forgiven you and offered you a second chance. I'm willing to do the same."

Kate smiled and pointed at the carafe. "That coffee smells delicious. I'll have a cup."

As Sara poured, Kate read notes from her phone. "Nina Girardin was born in Marseilles, France, and moved here when she was twenty-nine. She's forty-eight now, college educated, and the owner of a string of boutiques. As far as I could determine, the shops make money. At least, she has a great credit rating and no outstanding debt other than a mortgage."

"Do you know what she did while living in France?"

"She went to work for a fashion designer after leaving college. Prior to that she had done some modeling to pay her way through school."

"What about her marriage?"

"That ended in tragedy when her husband died of a heart attack. At the time, foul play was suspected."

Sara had been stirring her coffee. Her hand stopped moving as she stared over at Kate.

"Nina was suspected of killing him?"

"She was accused by her husband's older sister. The two women never got along. An autopsy proved that the man died of a heart attack and no charges were ever leveled against Miss Girardin. As a side note, I uncovered the fact that she buys flowers on her late husband's birthday. He's buried in Florida, and her travel records place her there at the same time each year. I would say that she's visiting his grave. I doubt she would do that if she'd killed him. It sounds more like the actions of a grieving widow."

"It does," Sara admitted. "Is there anything else of interest?"

"She has a half-brother who has been in and out of jail in France. He's currently serving a sentence for carjacking a woman after beating her into unconsciousness. It looks as though she never visits him."

"I don't blame her. Thank you for doing this. I'll tell Cody to pay you when he gets back."

"There's no need. We were well compensated for identifying Cyrus Daly, and we're still looking for him."

"Thank you. That man wants my father dead. He has to be found."

"Is Tanner with your father?"

"Yes."

"Then you don't have to worry. He'll keep him safe."

"I know he will. He already prevented a second killer from harming Daddy. I feel sick when I imagine what would have happened had Cody not been there."

Kate stayed a little longer before saying she had to get back to searching for Cyrus. As she was about to walk out, Sara asked her a question.

"Why didn't Michael come with you?"

Kate smiled. "He's scared of you, Sara. The last time we saw you, you looked as if you would have preferred to kill us rather than give us a second chance." Kate laughed. "You also made him clean toilets."

"A little honest work was good for him."

"He avoids it as much as possible," Kate admitted.

The elevator was still available from her arrival. Kate stepped on and sent Sara a wave goodbye.

THE KILL SQUAD CYRUS HIRED TO MURDER WARREN Blake had a secret—they were all young women.

Their leader was an ex-street walker named Barbara Jean. She was a twenty-two-year-old blonde with huge green eyes and a gapped-tooth smile. On her phone was an app that could change her voice, giving it a deep bass sound and making others believe she was a man.

She'd run away from a good home at sixteen after stealing from her parents to fund a trip to Hollywood. Barbara Jean had been certain that she had what it took to be a movie star. Instead, she fell into the clutches of a pimp named Fernando who got her hooked on meth. She turned tricks on the streets of LA for seven months. Her final night, two men robbed her, and when she had no money to give her pimp, he beat her so badly that he believed she was dead.

Fernando left her lying in an alley. She lay there for a full day before regaining consciousness and crawling out to the street where she was spotted and given help. The beating had altered something in Barbara Jean's mind. She had been a sweet, frightened girl before. Afterward, she was full of anger and lacked a sense of fear. All she could think about was getting revenge on her pimp.

Oddest of all, the massive craving for methamphetamines had left her. Whatever part of her brain signaled that desire had been damaged or transformed by the severe beating she'd taken.

While she was in the hospital receiving care for a cracked skull and a broken jaw, the police questioned her about the pimp. They were eager to put Fernando away for attempted murder. Barbara Jean told them that Fernando was innocent and that it was the men who had robbed her who had beaten her.

The police knew it was a lie but couldn't get her to change her story. They told her that her parents were coming to LA to take her home.

Her mother and father arrived, cried when they saw what condition she was in, and Barbara Jean returned to the small Georgia town she had fled months earlier.

She'd always been smart, so catching up at school hadn't been difficult. Her old friends stayed away as B.J., as they called her, was not the same girl they had known. There was a dangerous look in her large eyes that hadn't been there before. It went along with the faint scar on the right side of her forehead.

That was the spot Fernando had pounded with his fists.

She slowly gained back the weight she had lost while addicted. It gave her face a fuller look and another year of maturing added two inches of height to her.

High school graduation came along with Barbara Jean's eighteenth birthday. Her parents bought her a good used car as a gift. It was a vehicle she was supposed to use to drive back and forth to state college. Barbara Jean said goodbye to her parents and climbed into her car to head to freshman orientation. She never got there. Instead, she cleaned out the money in her college fund and headed to LA. On the way there, she dyed her hair dark and worked on eliminating her southern accent. She'd been practicing a new accent for a while and had adopted a speech pattern that made her sound like she was from Brooklyn. As an aspiring actress, she had labored on mimicking accents for years. She no longer wanted to be an actress, but the skill would come in handy.

FERNANDO WAS AT THE BUS STATION IN NORTH Hollywood. It had been weeks since he'd recruited a girl there. Oh, the Hollywood hopefuls still arrived every day, but he was not the only one looking for them. Several other pimps had moved in and beaten him to prime candidates; there were also the do-gooders who tried to keep the girls from winding up on the streets. Fernando had been in a slump, but that was about to change.

He spotted a girl with shoulder-length dark hair. She was wearing a pair of sunglasses and holding a suitcase. Fernando cursed as a pimp he knew approached the girl and started running his game. Like all pimps, the man was kind to the girl, hoping to win her trust.

The girl shot him down and made her way into a coffee shop. Fernando followed her in and began chatting her up. He wasn't handsome, but he had a charming manner that he could turn off and on at will. When he offered to pay for the girl's food so that she could save her money, she accepted.

Fernando asked her questions about herself and listened with rapt attention as if she were the most fascinating person he had ever met. The thought that there was something familiar about her flitted through his mind but never took hold. The girl's Brooklyn accent was one he had heard before but not recently. It was the large green eyes he decided. They made him think of that southern bitch he had beaten the snot out of the year before. That had been necessary to keep the other girls from thinking they could hide money from him and claim that they had been robbed. A little violence was needed every once in a while to keep order. Fernando also found it to be a rush.

When the girl, Cindy she said her name was, mentioned that she had nowhere to stay, Fernando told her that he had a friend who owned a hotel nearby. His friend would let her have a room at a discount. When Cindy touched him on the arm and told him he was so nice, he knew he had her.

BARBARA JEAN FOUND THE HOTEL TO BE EVEN SEEDIER than she'd remembered. It was a three-story building that had eight rooms on each floor. Fernando insisted on helping her out by paying for the room, because he knew she needed to save her money.

After opening the door for her he carried in her suitcase. "You can pay me back for everything when you become famous."

Barbara Jean had laughed at that, and while she laughed, she gripped the Taser she had in her purse.

"I'll pay you back right now, Fernando."

The twin barbs of the Taser sank into the side of Fernando's neck. He went down to the floor, falling on the suitcase. Barbara Jean's hand fished into her purse again and removed a set of handcuffs she had bought at a sex shop while passing through Las Vegas. With Fernando's wrists bound behind him, she dipped into the purse once more and brought out duct tape and a rag to gag him with.

Fernando was recovering from the shock he'd received and tried to bite her as she stuffed the rag in his mouth. He missed her fingers and she proceeded to secure the gag using the tape.

He resisted violently as she tried to tape his ankles together. A hard kick to the testicles ended that long enough for her to bind the ankles. When she was done, Barbara Jean spoke to him in her own voice. As Fernando heard the soft southern lilt his eyes went wide.

"You do remember me? I'm so glad. I was beginning to wonder."

Fernando struggled against his bonds as he released a string of what Barbara Jean assumed were muffled curses and threats. She patted him on the cheek.

"Save your energy, Fernando," she said while laughing, "you're gonna need it." She grabbed up her suitcase and tossed it on the bed. Inside the case was an assortment of modern torture devices. Barbara Jean had acquired them at the same sex shop where she had bought the handcuffs. The store had an extensive bondage and sadomasochism section.

Barbara Jean still smiled whenever she remembered the look on the store clerk's face as he was ringing up her selections.

Over the next seven hours she gave Fernando a taste of hell before sending him there for real. He finally died after being beaten to death with a hammer.

IN THE MONTHS THAT FOLLOWED, BARBARA JEAN HAD made her living killing pimps like Fernando. Fernando himself had revealed where he stashed his money and Barbara Jean had left LA with over thirty thousand dollars and a load of jewelry and watches.

She had been hoping for more cash, but Fernando had been a coke head who wasted money eating out all the time and gambling.

Barbara Jean gained a partner in crime after saving a girl with long dark hair who was being beaten by a pimp in San Francisco. The girl, Deidre, was new to town and had insulted the pimp. Unlike the young Barbara Jean, sixteen-year-old Deidre wasn't a wide-eyed innocent. She looked older than she was and often passed for a college student. Deidre had run away from home, though, because she was avoiding being charged with the murder of her stepfather, who had tried to rape her.

Barbara Jean took the girl under her wing and they became a team. It had been Deidre's idea to start killing for money.

"Pimp's have money," Barbara Jean had argued.

"Yeah, but you have to torture them to get it. I'm not all into that shit like you are. A clean shot to the head is better, quicker, and we might make more."

"Who would hire us?"

"They'll find us online. Back home I had a boyfriend who used to hire himself out to get revenge for other people. The worst thing he ever did was beat up some guy with a baseball bat. I was there when he did it. He threw up afterward, but I liked it."

Barbara Jean agreed to try it. They had their first client three weeks later. She was a woman in Portland, Oregon. She wanted her cheating husband killed so that she could get his life insurance. Deidre let the guy pick her up in a bar one night and led him to a motel room. They were both drunk.

Barbara Jean wasn't drunk, and when the guy entered the room, she hit him hard across the face with a steering wheel she had bought for salvage at a junk yard. It broke the man's nose and knocked him out. The steering wheel was from the same model car that the man drove, a vintage Mustang. She hoped by using it that it would help avoid raising red flags during an autopsy. They were planning to make it look like the man died after crashing his car.

Deidre, although inebriated, was sober enough to help load the man into the passenger seat of his Mustang. Deidre sat in the rear as Barbara Jean drove to an area they had picked out earlier, and where they had stashed a vehicle. It was the route the man routinely took when driving home from the bar.

After placing him behind the wheel and positioning the car just right, Barbara Jean reached through the open window and placed the car in gear. It drove forward and slipped over a hill. When it reached bottom, it smashed into a stand of trees.

As Deidre waited for her, Barbara Jean went down the hill to check on their victim. He was dead, having gone through the windshield. Barbara Jean cursed. She had been sure that she would have found him slumped over the steering wheel, which was why she'd gone to the trouble of buying one like it to strike him with. Hell, she could have just used a rock.

Seven contracts and nine months later they came across two sisters who were in the same line of work. Late one night, while looking for a good place to bury their next victim, Barbara Jean and Deidre came upon Callie and Cassandra as they were disposing of a body.

They had come close to shooting each other that

night. Callie, the oldest sister at twenty-one, had thought they were cops looking to arrest them. Once she realized that Barbara Jean and Deidre were no threat, Callie suggested that they talk.

The women became friends, and later accomplices, while taking on more difficult contracts. Being young and attractive, they had the advantage of being underestimated by their primarily male victims. It gave them the huge advantage of surprise in every encounter. Cassandra, like Deidre, was into computers. Their skill enabled them to acquire contracts without ever having to meet their clients.

Once, a client turned out to be a police detective working in a New Orleans cybercrime division. The contract had been placed on a fictional business partner that had to die in a way that appeared accidental. Callie, a redhead, had been sent into the man's office while pretending to be looking for work.

She was supposed to flirt with him and have him agree to meet with her later over drinks. Online, the client, the cybercrimes cop, had told her that the best time to make contact with the target was at two p.m.

Callie had arrived fifteen minutes early, figuring that she could wait in the lobby if needed. She never got in to see the man playing the part of the phony target. Instead, the receptionist, an undercover policewoman, flashed her badge at her and asked her to leave the building.

"Try coming back tomorrow, hon. The real management will be here then. Good luck with the job hunting."

Callie left the building, and after rounding a corner, ran away. She knew how close she had come to being caught. Had anyone checked her purse they would have found an unlicensed gun and a set of handcuffs.

The police were so convinced that they were laying a trap for a man that a young woman like Callie wasn't even on their radar. Since that time, the women had taken extra precautions not to get caught.

Although they knew where Blake was and assumed that he was being guarded by only one man, they had to make certain that it wasn't a police or FBI sting operation. They spent a day exploring the area and looking for signs that there was increased police activity. They found nothing but a bunch of small-town cops going about their usual day-to-day business. There were no sedans with federal tags parked in their lots and no one in the area's eateries was gossiping about a group of strangers. Barbara Jean and the others were satisfied that they were safe to proceed.

～

Barbara Jean studied one of the motion detectors Tanner had put in place around the cabin. It had been hidden among bushes but not impossible to find if someone knew to look for it. She and the others had plans to approach the cabin around eight a.m.

The four of them were dressed like hikers, sexy hikers, as they wore shorts and tops that revealed their bare midriffs. Cassandra kept her auburn locks styled short, but the others all had long hair. It hung down past their shoulders and moved about in the soft spring breeze.

Deidre predicted that Warren Blake and his bodyguard would be fantasizing about them right up until the time they shot them dead. If so, they wouldn't be the first of their victims to have done so.

"Well?" Deidre asked.

"This motion detector isn't police issue; it is high quality," Barbara Jean said. "I also think we would have come across someone by now if this was a trap set by the cops. Blake has only one bodyguard. The police would have filled these woods with people."

"I agree," Cassandra said. "We'll move in. Everyone keep an eye out."

"Remember," Barbara Jean said, "we take them alive if we get the chance. Blake must have money stashed somewhere, the bodyguard might too. There's no sense in leaving that to some damn relative or the tax man."

Deidre laughed. "Not everyone is a pimp with a hidden stash, B.J."

"I know. But it doesn't hurt to find out. Remember that real estate agent we killed in Colorado last year? The guy had sixty grand hidden in his basement. If we hadn't tortured him first, we would have missed it."

The other women nodded their agreement. They moved left, leaving the obvious footpath and ducking behind the bushes that had obscured the motion detector. The cabin was close, but they had left their vehicle over a mile away. They hadn't parked any closer for fear that the sound of the car's engine might have carried.

TANNER HAD RISEN EARLY AND DRESSED IN A PAIR OF black cotton shorts to workout. He couldn't go for a run and leave Warren unprotected, so he did an intense calisthenics routine in the living room instead. It was ninety minutes of high-energy movements that used his own bodyweight for resistance. By the time he was done, he was sweating freely.

Warren had risen as Tanner was finishing up with alternating sets of one-arm handstand push-ups. It was an exhibition of great strength and supreme balance. When he was finished and transitioned to a standing position in one fluid motion, Warren shook his head in amazement.

"There are professional athletes who aren't in as good condition as you are."

"That's because their lives don't depend on it. If they had to steal second base or die, they would take their workouts to a whole other level."

"I'll bring the dog inside while you shower."

"He's gone. He chewed through the rope and is off in the woods. Hopefully he'll return later."

"I'll fry up some bacon. If he's near enough to smell it, he'll come back," Warren said.

"I won't be in the shower for long but keep an eye out. If you see someone, give me a shout and let me know."

"I will, but I'd bet there's not another person around for miles."

"You're probably right," Tanner said. He entered the bathroom and laid the shotgun on the sink, then began undressing.

TANNER WAS UNDER THE SPRAY OF THE SHOWER WHEN Warren decided to go outside and grab a few pieces of firewood. The weather had been mild, but he still liked the atmosphere that a fire produced.

He stooped to examine the frayed end of the rope Lucky had chewed through. He hoped the hound returned. It had been nice having him around.

"Hello."

Warren jerked his head up in surprise at the sound of the voice. When he saw the four young women, he waved in greeting. They were backpackers by the look of them. They had just emerged from the trees and were walking toward him. He smiled and called out to them.

"Hi. Are you ladies camping nearby?"

"Something like that," Deidre said. She continued to smile at Warren, as her hand freed a Glock from the holster secured at her back.

NAKED CAME THE DANGER

CYRUS HAD ATTEMPTED TO USE A DISPOSABLE RAZOR to shave his head the night before. He wound up nicking his scalp and drawing blood, so he abandoned the effort. Meanwhile, his hair was growing back faster than he would have imagined, making him look more like his old self.

The private plane he'd chartered would be available in the afternoon, just a few hours away. He didn't want to risk being recognized when he was so close to getting away for good. He'd decided he would return to the barbershop where he'd had his hair shaved off and have them do it again.

But first, he wanted to wait for the call to come in confirming that Warren Blake was dead. He was hopeful that the job would finally get done, although he did have a backup plan ready to go. Cyrus had heard from the Russian assassin he'd sent a down payment to. The man was eager to get the contract and was already in the United States.

Cyrus had typed a question to him.

You flew here from Russia just on the chance that I would hire you?

No. I already had a contract set up in Chicago.

I may not need you. There is a group of four going after Blake. He should be dead by noon.

Understood, but I am ready if needed. Deposit the rest of my fee and consider the lawyer dead.

Cyrus rolled his eyes upon reading that last statement. He'd heard similar promises issued before. The latest declaration had been by the leader of the hit squad he'd hired. Then again, the ones who had failed had been lone assassins, a group of four killers should finally get the job done. Cyrus looked at the upper right-hand corner of his laptop screen for the time. It was 7:56 a.m.

WARREN BLAKE WAS A RESPECTED MEMBER OF THE bar, had run for public office, was approaching sixty, and was a grandfather of two young children. He was still a man. Seeing four beautiful and shapely young women walking toward him was a pleasant experience, to say the least.

The one speaking to him, Deidre, Warren found to be the most striking of all, with her long raven hair, turquoise eyes, and large breasts. Deidre was showing a good portion of cleavage that Warren was trying not to stare at as he started down the porch steps to greet them. When the woman brought her hand out from behind her back and he saw that it was holding a gun, Warren realized he'd been lured into a trap by beauty.

A cry that was a mixture of shock and panic broke from his throat. The sudden halting of his forward motion caused him to stumble and fall against the wooden railing. Deidre was less than twenty feet away and taking aim at his chest.

KA-BLAM!

The sound of a shotgun blast reverberated in the air as the screen door behind Warren exploded. The pellets that obliterated the screen kept going and burrowed their way into Deidre's face, exited through the back of her shattered skull, and finally struck Callie in the throat.

What was left of the screen door was shoved open and Tanner emerged holding the shotgun that had killed Deidre. He was naked, his hair was wet, and shampoo still streaked it white with suds.

Tanner had been in the shower when he'd heard Warren call out a greeting to someone. Because of the sound of the shower water he couldn't quite make out the words. He had the shower door open and was reaching for the shotgun when he'd heard Deidre's response. The fact that it was the voice of a young woman hadn't lessened his concern one iota.

Cassandra had slipped her weapon out and was holding it loosely at her side. She had become distracted with concern by the blood flowing from her sister's neck wound and looked frozen into inaction. Tanner helped get her moving by sending a load of double-ought buckshot into her midsection. That sent Cassandra stumbling backwards to tumble onto the ground. Her weapon left her hand and landed several feet away.

BARBARA JEAN'S MIND WAS SCREAMING SEVERAL things at her at once.

DEIDRE'S DEAD!

THE SISTERS ARE WOUNDED!

THERE'S A NAKED MAN!

FIRE YOUR DAMN GUN!

RUN!

Barbara Jean decided to run and shoot at the same time. It should have been a recipe for disaster since she was shooting as she turned to find cover and her aim was off by several yards. Instead, fortune favored her. She fired three shots. Her first bullet sailed over the hood of the pickup truck, while a second one tore into the vehicle's radiator. The third and final round proved to be blessed with luck. It struck the metal bumper on the old Ford pickup. That slug then ricocheted into Tanner's shotgun with enough force to drive it from his hands. The weapon clattered down the steps and fell onto the ground.

Tanner was rushing down the stairs to reclaim it when Barbara Jean sent two rounds into the ground near the shotgun.

"Try and pick it up again and I'll kneecap you."

TANNER STRAIGHTENED, AND WHILE DOING SO HE considered his options. They were few and not to his liking. His best chance at saving Warren and himself was to risk charging Barbara Jean. She would get at least one shot off, but if he was fast enough and hit her right the shot might not strike anything vital. If he could grab her wrist and angle the gun, he might escape with a leg wound. A bullet to the leg could certainly kill, but it was better than taking one to the head or heart.

BARBARA JEAN HAD REGAINED CONTROL OF HERSELF. She hadn't been so frightened since the night that Fernando had nearly beaten her to death. She hated the feeling. Now that she was the only one with a weapon, she felt herself grow calm. Despite how badly everything had just gone, she could still salvage something. The naked bodyguard looked threatening even unarmed, but the lawyer, Blake, appeared stunned into inaction. Blake was seated on a step and holding onto the wooden handrail as if it were a life preserver. She decided she would torture and kill him last.

She looked down at the dead form of Deidre and felt the loss. The girl had been her best friend. Callie and Cassandra were severely wounded. There was so much blood around Cassandra that Barbara Jean was sure she'd be dead within minutes. She likely was already. The wound to her stomach had done malicious things to her insides. Anyone with such wounds should be wailing in agony. Cassandra was silent, and still.

Callie was a bloody mess as well. The left side of her white tube top had turned red from the wound in her neck. She was on her back and looking up at Barbara Jean while panting away as if she had been running. Blood was leaking from her neck, not spurting. It was possible she could be saved. Barbara Jean frowned. She and Callie got along but weren't that close, so of course she's the one who would live.

"Hey you, bodyguard. Do you have first aid training?"

"I do," Tanner said.

"Then help my friend."

Tanner began moving closer to Barbara Jean. He did so while pretending to look over at Callie to assess her wound. When he looked back at Barbara Jean, he saw that her gaze was directed below his waist.

"You're quite the man, bodyguard," Barbara Jean said as she gathered up the fallen shotgun. The slug that had knocked it out of Tanner's hands left a gouge mark along its metal stock. Barbara Jean was examining the indentation while smiling. She had become distracted. It was the opening Tanner had been hoping for. He had been about to attack, but then he relaxed and spoke to her.

"Lucky," Tanner said.

Barbara Jean laughed. "That ricochet off the truck's bumper? Hell yeah, it was lucky."

Tanner shook his head. "I was talking to the dog."

Barbara Jean heard a growl and the scampering of paws an instant before Lucky slammed into her from behind. She went down on her knees, then cried out in pain as Lucky bit her on the back of her arm.

Tanner sent a barefooted kick into her face that split her upper lip and broke her nose. After that, disarming her was easy. Barbara Jean was squirming along the ground as she tried to get away from the dog. Lucky kept at her, growling and biting. Tanner got ahold of the loose end of rope still dangling from the Lab's collar and pulled him away from Barbara Jean. When he looked over at Callie, he saw a pair of sightless eyes staring back at him.

Tears of pain streamed down Barbara Jean's cheeks as she sat up. "Keep that animal away from me!"

"Come get the dog, Warren. I want you and Lucky to go inside the house."

Warren walked over with a still stunned expression on his face. "I… they looked like hikers, college kids."

"I understand. It's all right. Go inside while I finish this."

"Finish?" Warren said.

"She can't be allowed to live."

"Oh, good Lord."

"Go inside. I'll be right in."

Warren pulled Lucky past the ravaged screen door and inside the house. The dog whined, as he wanted to stay by Tanner's side. Tanner leveled the shotgun at Barbara Jean. She held up a pleading hand.

"You don't have to kill me. Look at me. Look at my body. It's nice, right? I'll do anything you want if you let me—"

Barbara Jean died, and Tanner went inside to get dressed.

17

BAD DUDE, GOOD MAN

THE JAPANESE ASSASSIN, TARAN, LOOKED CONFUSED as he left New Hampshire and entered Maine while driving along I-95. The sign at the border had the message, MAINE – WELCOME HOME.

Taran reasoned that surely there were many people who drove into the state who were not returning natives. It made no sense to welcome them home as if they had always lived there.

He placed the matter in a mental file he had labeled *Idiosyncrasies of American Culture* and checked his progress on the vehicle's GPS. It let him know that he was about three hours away from Warren Blake's cabin.

He had already checked out the vacant rental property and staked out the home of the woman Blake was seeing, Nina Girardin. When he failed to find evidence that the lawyer was present at either location, he realized he should have first checked to determine if Blake's plane were missing from its assigned hangar at a regional airport. The plane was gone, which indicated that Blake had flown to Maine. Six hours later, Taran was riding along a Maine highway. He was aware that other assassins were looking for Blake, and that they wanted to kill him. Taran wondered if the trip would be a waste of time and he would find only a dead man.

NOON CAME AND WENT WITHOUT CYRUS HEARING from Barbara Jean. At one o'clock he released a great weary sigh. Warren Blake was still alive, and yet more money had been wasted trying to kill him.

He debated hiring the Russian only because of the amount of money that was needed. He sent the payment moments later along with a warning that Blake's bodyguard was deadly.

He still had millions of Zander Hall's money left, enough to live off for the rest of his life, and he knew he would feel like crap if he let Hall down.

The Russian wasn't quite his last hope. Cyrus had sent off another message to the go-between who had contact with the Japanese assassin Taran. A man of

Taran's reputation would get a fortune for the hit. His message had been ignored.

Cyrus wasn't displeased by the snub. If he had to pay Taran he would have been left with little of Hall's money to fund his new life. If the Russian failed, Cyrus decided he would establish himself in his new life, then make the trip back to the East Coast someday to kill Blake himself. Maybe he should have done so in the beginning when Blake was ignorant that he was a target.

He was about to pack up his things in the suitcase when he decided to leave it all behind. He didn't need any of it and would start over from scratch once he made it to San Francisco. His itchy scalp reminded him that he needed to have his head shaved again; Cyrus checked out of his hotel room and headed to the barbershop.

~

TANNER HAD LOADED THE BODIES OF BARBARA JEAN and her crew into the pickup truck's bed. Before doing so, he had lined the truck bed with plastic garbage bags.

He and Warren drove along an old logging trail deeper into the woods, searching for a place to dispose of them. The truck was still usable despite the leak at the midway point in its radiator. It was running hot and would need to be fed more water before making a return trip to the cabin. It would have time to cool down while they performed their unpleasant tasks.

Warren apologized once more for endangering Tanner by not letting him know that someone had approached the cabin.

"I would have never thought those women were killers."

"That was their main advantage. I'm sure they were successful assassins because of it."

Warren shuddered. "I thought I was dead when she pointed that gun at me. If you hadn't... thank you, Cody. Once again you've saved my life."

"You're welcome, but we can't stay here any longer. There's no telling who else Cyrus might send after you, and it's possible he was given this location."

"Where will we go?"

"I have an idea. I'll need to make a call when we're done here."

Lucky was seated between them. Warren petted the dog. "This hound was certainly named well. We might have both died if he hadn't attacked that woman."

"I was surprised to see him return to the cabin, given all the gunfire."

They arrived at the end of the trail to an open

area that had been cleared of trees decades earlier. In the years since, the forest had reclaimed some of it with plants and wild shrubs. Here and there, copse of trees had taken root as well. Given enough time, it would be as if the older trees had never been cut down.

Tanner climbed to the top of a nearby hill and spent several minutes scanning their surroundings through a pair of binoculars. The spot he was in sat between two trees that were the only ones on the hill. He saw no one. It was a weekday. That reduced the possibility of coming across hikers and others seeking recreation in the wilderness.

He had told Warren to dress in clothes he wouldn't miss, as they would have to burn their garments later, that included shoes.

After finding a spot that seemed unlikely to draw anyone's attention, Tanner began digging. Barbara Jean, Deidre, Cassandra, and Callie were going in the ground.

Warren wanted to help dig, and Tanner let him. If anyone came near, Lucky would let them know.

TANNER SPENT THE LAST HOUR DIGGING ALONE, AS Warren was spent from the effort and his hands had begun to bleed despite the work gloves he'd been wearing. Tanner told him to rest. The lawyer had held up better than most would have in his situation, and although fit, he was not a young man.

Much of the time spent digging required the removal of stones in the soil, but at last, Tanner had a hole that was deep enough to accommodate four bodies. He'd climbed out of the grave and went to the pickup. The bodies were in the bed under a tarp, along with their weapons.

They hadn't come across the vehicle the women had arrived in, nor did they have the time to search for it. Whatever vehicle they had used, the women had likely stolen it. Tanner assumed it had been parked off-road under a stand of trees somewhere.

If not for Warren, he would have taken off on foot to find it. Unlike the pickup truck, the women's car wouldn't limp along with a leaking radiator. But if he left Warren to search for the vehicle, another assassin might come along. There were old logging and mining roads scattered about the area, some within a short hike in several directions. The women might have also hidden the car with camouflage or natural cover such as tree branches. Tanner might find it within an hour or search in vain for a full day. It didn't matter; they would be flying out before nightfall.

TANNER BACKED THE PICKUP AS CLOSE TO THE EDGE of the hole as he could get it and killed the engine. Warren approached, but Tanner waved him off.

"I'll handle it."

"I can help."

"Not with this. Please Warren, take a seat in the truck."

Warren was about to protest when Tanner pulled back the tarp and revealed the bodies, along with the disturbing sight came strong odors of blood, urine, and feces. The lawyer gagged and turned his back. Once he was seated inside the truck, Tanner went to work unloading the corpses. It disturbed him as well. These were the bodies of young women. It seemed unnatural that they should have died so early in life and in such a manner.

They had left him no choice. They had forfeited their lives when they decided to try to kill Sara's father. Tanner had promised his wife that Warren would remain safe. He would keep that promise even if it cost him his own life.

Once Tanner had a layer of soil covering the women, Warren returned, grabbed a shovel, and helped to fill in the grave. They worked in silence.

Tanner refilled the broken radiator with water poured from two jugs. The liquid seemed to be dripping out at a faster pace than earlier.

On the trip back to the cabin, Warren had a question.

"Have you had to do something like that often?"

"I've done it before."

"You've chosen a hell of a way to live your life. I also think you're uniquely suited for it. You're as hard a man as I've ever known, and believe me, being a defense attorney, I've had dealings with hard men. Despite that, you've managed to hold on to your humanity. I've watched you with Lucas and Sara. They couldn't ask for a more loving father or husband."

"I'm like everyone else, Warren. I'm a result of my circumstances and decisions. When my family was wiped out by killers, instead of hiding and fearing people like that for the rest of my life, I vowed to be better at killing than they were. I won't ever apologize for who I am."

Warren slowed the truck and brought it to a stop. "Cody, son, I wasn't chastising you. I'm in awe of you. When Sara said she was marrying a hired killer I admit I thought she was making a mistake she would regret for the rest of her life, and I told her as much. Do you know what she said to me?"

"What?"

"She said that yes, you were a hired killer and a murderer many times over, but you were also the best man she knew, next to me." Warren smiled. "I think she threw that last part in just so she wouldn't hurt my feelings."

"Sara's opinions about me have always been extreme, one way or another."

Warren extended his arm past Lucky and clapped him on the shoulder. "But she was right. You are a damn good man, and I'm proud that you're a part of our family."

Tanner cleared his throat. "Thank you."

Warren got the truck moving again. "I'll never forget this trip to the cabin, that's for damn sure."

Tanner smiled. "No, I guess you wouldn't."

18

HOW ABOUT A RIDE?

THE BARBER, ANGELO, WOULDN'T HAVE REALIZED HE had seen Cyrus before if Cyrus hadn't asked the man to shave his head again.

The man in the photo Adamo Conti had given him had blue eyes. The barber had remembered those eyes because of their brilliant color. The man taking a seat in his chair had brown eyes and wore glasses. But there were those rosy red cheeks of Cyrus's. Despite the change in eye color, those cheeks stood out and were memorable. As he pretended to be changing a blade on his clipper, the barber sent off a text.

The man you want is here.

THE RUSSIAN ASSASSIN WAS NAMED BORIS SOKOLOV. He had once been an aspiring actor and had a knack for mimicking speech patterns, accents, and mannerisms. He was also a master of disguise. These attributes should have combined to make him into a star of stage and screen. However, despite Sokolov's overabundance of talents as a thespian, he possessed a fatal flaw—the man could never remember his lines. Needless to say, that was not a good trait for an actor.

He still loved acting, and he would often entertain his friends at his local bar by doing different accents and impersonations of celebrities. Once, he took the time to make himself up to resemble their Finnish bartender. No one caught on that he wasn't really the bartender until the actual man showed up for work.

"It's like looking at twins, Boris," said one of his friends. "How do you do that? You normally look and sound nothing like him?"

"It's only a hobby," Sokolov said sadly.

There was someone in the bar who took note of Sokolov's talents. He was an older man who dressed well and wore an expensive watch. He had thought of a way Sokolov could put his talents to use without having to remember a bunch of dialog and stage directions. That man had been an assassin. He recruited Sokolov to act as a decoy and distraction.

Sokolov was reluctant to get involved in anything criminal. That is, until the man mentioned how much he could make for pretending to be one of the guards of a target he was after.

Sokolov went to work transforming himself into a double of the lead bodyguard of a Leningrad mobster. He visited the restaurant where the man ate breakfast and listened as the guard discussed a soccer match with a friend. He went home afterward to practice and by noon he was able to sound like the bodyguard.

Three nights later, Sokolov strode up to the front door of the home where the mob figure lived and spoke to the men guarding him that night. All three took him to be their boss. Sokolov not only looked like the man, but he had his slouching posture, and was scratching at his beard every few seconds the way the man routinely did. The fake beard was a match for the gray-streaked one the real head bodyguard wore.

"Go take a break, guys."

The men looked at each other, then back at him.

"You want us to leave?" one of them asked.

"I'll still be here. And Alexey should arrive soon."

"Who's Alexey?" one of the men asked.

Sokolov had meant to say the name Anatoly. He never could remember even the simplest of lines.

"Anatoly, I should have said Anatoly. He'll be here soon with Dimitri."

"We should wait until they get here?" one of the other men said.

Sokolov spoke in an authoritative tone. "Go now. But be back within an hour."

The men left the home and drove off. Sokolov walked through the house and opened a rear door to let in his deadly employer. When he asked if he could witness the murder, the assassin stared at him with surprise registering on his face.

"I thought you would be eager to leave."

"Why?"

"Fear. But you're not afraid to be here, are you?"

"I did my part and the guards are gone. What's to fear?"

The assassin smiled. "You and I will do well together."

The contract was fulfilled a minute later as Sokolov watched. The head bodyguard was named a traitor and killed the next day, despite his assertions of innocence. For his trouble, Sokolov received more money than he made in months at the factory where he worked. He never went back to the factory, nor even bothered to claim his final measly paycheck.

∾

IN THE YEARS THAT FOLLOWED, SOKOLOV REALIZED HE could make much more money if he did the killing himself. He had taken lives as a young soldier in Afghanistan and never lost sleep over it. Presently, his abilities as an actor and an assassin were better than they'd ever been.

Cyrus had informed him that the last he'd heard, Warren Blake was hiding out at a cabin in Maine. A simple check of property records online resulted in Sokolov learning the address of the cabin.

Cyrus Daly had also warned him that Blake's bodyguard was lethal. That aggression would be directed at others, not at a man he believed to be his employer. Sokolov would impersonate Blake, and once the bodyguard turned his back on him, Sokolov would place a bullet in his head.

TANNER AND WARREN WERE READY TO LEAVE MAINE. As they walked toward the converted garage that acted as a hangar for the Cessna, Tanner realized that they might not be going anywhere.

"We could have a problem," Tanner said, as he pointed at a small hole in the side of the structure. The first shot Barbara Jean fired had sailed over the hood of the pickup truck and struck the hangar.

Warren swung back one door as Tanner opened

the other, while Lucky stood by watching them. They both felt relief when they saw nothing of immediate concern.

"I don't see anything leaking," Warren said. "That's a good sign."

Tanner studied the hole left in the hangar wall, followed its trajectory, then pointed at the plane.

"There's a hole at the bottom of the aircraft, beneath the wing."

Warren grabbed a toolbox that was sitting on a wooden table. Tanner took out a wrench, crawled beneath the plane and went to work opening an access panel. He needed a flashlight to find the damage. It was there. Barbara Jean's bullet had frayed a section of the flight control cable. The slug wasn't in view and could have damaged something else out of sight.

When Warren slid beneath the plane to look, he let out a curse. "We won't be flying out tonight. It's too risky."

"I agree," Tanner said. "Even if we wanted to chance flying with a frayed cable, we don't know what else might have been damaged."

"We can still ride out in the truck and make it into town."

"We're better off here. In town, I would have no way of knowing who could be a threat or just another hotel guest or visitor. Anyone showing up here didn't just happen by. If they're here, they're here to kill you."

"Like those women," Warren said softly.

"Yeah."

They closed up the hangar and headed inside the cabin. Since they were staying, Tanner built a fire, while Warren restarted the generator.

"We'll ride out tomorrow, early," Tanner said. "Once we're in town, we'll get the radiator on the truck fixed. Then we'll drive somewhere to rent a car."

"There are aviation mechanics in the area; we could get the plane fixed. I once noticed I had an aileron stuck in an upward position while doing a preflight inspection. They sent a man out the next day to work on it."

"That's no good. Bringing a mechanic out here could endanger them."

Warren's lips parted slightly as he thought that over. "You're right. I hadn't considered that."

"I'm going to stay awake tonight and keep watch. I'll be doing it outside. I don't want to take a chance on anyone getting as close to you as that last group did."

"When will you sleep, Cody?"

"I'll be fine. I've gone without sleep before."

Warren reached over and petted Lucky. "I'm glad

our new friend came back. He'll let us know if someone is coming."

"Let's eat early. After that, I'll begin my watch."

"I wish I could take over and let you sleep some."

"We could be in for a quiet night. Cyrus Daly might still be waiting to hear what happened. By the time he figures out you survived, we'll no longer be here."

"Or better yet, the police have caught up with him."

Tanner smiled. "I have other people looking for him. If they find him, he'll wish he had turned himself in to the cops."

ANGELO THE BARBER HAD TAKEN HIS TIME SHAVING Cyrus's head, but he could only stall for so long and eventually finished the task. He had told his assistant barber to put the closed sign on the door so no other customers would walk in. He also gave the man the rest of the day off. The door was left unlocked, as Angelo was expecting Adamo Conti to show.

Angelo had seen Cyrus's photo on the news and knew the police were also looking for Cyrus and had accused him of murder. It had made Angelo glad he was holding a razor. He could defend himself if needed.

"Would you like me to shave your face too, sir?"

"No. I took care of that this morning."

Angelo had no choice but to remove the barber cape covering Cyrus so that he could pay and leave. He had just removed the cape from his client when the bell above the door chimed, announcing Conti's arrival.

Adamo was not alone. Joe Pullo was with him. Pullo strode into the shop as if he owned it. In that way, the crooks and cops of Manhattan were alike. New York was their city, lock, stock, and barrel. They moved about its streets with confidence and self-assurance.

Pullo climbed into the barber chair to the left of the one Cyrus was seated in and swiveled it around to face him.

"Do you know who I am?"

Cyrus stared at him, and yes, there was something familiar about Pullo.

"I've seen you before... maybe on TV?"

"I'm Joe Pullo. You're Cyrus Daly. You made a big mistake by going after Warren Blake."

Cyrus stared at Pullo, then looked over at Adamo Conti, who stood by the door. He sprung out of the barber chair as if he'd been ejected, nearly fell as his shoes slipped on the polished floor, then bolted through a curtain and into a back room.

Angelo started after Cyrus but was halted by Pullo. "Let him go."

"He'll get away."

Joe smiled. "No, he won't."

As Cyrus passed through the curtain and into the back room his eyes searched for a way out. When he spotted the back door that led to an alley, he released a small laugh. His hands fumbled at the two locks on the door because of his eagerness to get away. When he looked over his shoulder, he was relieved to see that Pullo and his man had yet to catch up to him.

With the door open, Cyrus rushed out of the shop. He had been building up speed to sprint out to the street but stopped dead when he saw the man pointing a gun at him. The man's name was Finn Kelly. He smiled at Cyrus.

"Where are you rushing off to, lad? Perhaps I can give you a lift?"

Inside the barbershop, Joe was thanking Angelo for his help.

Angelo stuttered as he spoke to Pullo. "My, my,

my pleasure, Mr. Pullo, sir."

Pullo looked around. "I remember being here before, back when Sam was running things. Who owned the shop then?"

"That, that was my grandfather."

"I thought you might be related. You look like the guy I remember from back then." Pullo glanced over at Conti. "Is he paid up?"

"Yeah. Angelo is never a problem."

Joe reached into an inside pocket of his suit jacket and took out an envelope. "I appreciate your help." He held the envelope out to Angelo. Angelo stood frozen for a moment, but then took it. It was thick with hundred-dollar bills.

"Thank, thank you, Mr. Pullo, sir."

"You're welcome," Joe said, as he stared at Angelo. The envelope contained five thousand dollars. It was a nice sum but only a fraction of what Angelo and his family had paid in protection money over the decades their shop had been in business. Pullo couldn't imagine thanking someone for throwing him a bone after they'd systematically stolen the whole chicken from him. He sighed inwardly. That was life. There were wolves and there were sheep. Pullo came from a long line of wolves.

He left the shop with Adamo and walked to the curb where Red had the limo waiting. In the rear were Finn and Cyrus Daly. Cyrus was slumped down in his seat. His freshly shaved head gleamed.

"If you let me live, I can call off the dogs. There's an assassin out to kill Blake. I can stop him."

"How?" Joe said.

"I'll send a message."

"Then do it."

Cyrus nodded at Finn, who was seated across from him. "He took my phone."

"Let him have it back, Finn."

Cyrus was given his phone. He sent off a text to Sokolov, telling him to abort the contract and keep the money. After two minutes, it became clear that there would not be an immediate response.

"He'll see the message and leave Blake alone. He might also want to call me and hear me tell him that it's okay. If you kill me, he might carry out the contract."

"It doesn't matter," Joe said. "He won't kill Blake. Tanner is guarding Blake."

"Tanner? Is that the bodyguard's name? Is he one of your men?"

"I'm talking about Tanner the hit man. That's who's guarding Warren Blake."

"You mean he's real?"

Joe laughed. "He's real all right. I've a feeling you'll be meeting him soon."

Cyrus breathed a sigh of relief. "You're not going to kill me?"

"We're going to put you on ice. That doesn't mean you should plan on living a long life."

"I... I could pay you. I can give you millions if you'll just let me go."

"Yeah, you'll be giving up the money too before we're done with you."

Panic flared in Cyrus's eyes. Cyrus made a lunge toward Finn with the intention of yanking Finn's gun from the shoulder holster he was wearing. Finn put a stop to that by sending five hard jabs into Cyrus's face. The blows were so fast that they were nothing but a blur. The bald man with the rosy red cheeks moaned and fell to the floor of the limo.

"Thanks, Finn," Joe said. "I was tired of hearing him talk."

FINAL PERFORMANCE

Sokolov could make himself look like Warren Blake, sound like Warren Blake, and mimic Blake's mannerisms, but he could not lose twelve pounds in a matter of days or gain an inch and a half of height.

He was shorter than the lawyer and heavier. The weight was the result of his last hit in Chicago, where he'd had to gain pounds to better match the body shape of the man he'd been imitating.

Because of his skill at impersonation, the height and weight discrepancies didn't matter. Although, if he'd had more time to prepare, he would have lost the weight, bought lifts for his shoes, and attended to other minor details that would essentially make him Blake's double. At night, in the dark, with adrenalin pumping and anxiety churning, Blake's bodyguard would be fooled. There was no need to go to extreme measures.

While on a five-hour flight from Chicago to Bangor, Maine, Sokolov had studied interviews Blake had given on TV and at press conferences. He had learned to speak English long ago and was a master at imitating a southern accent, a Texas twang, or the nasal tone of a Bostonian. Blake's rather featureless voice would be easy to imitate.

He'd seen Cyrus's text and ignored it. He was committed to fulfilling the contract and his fee had already been paid. Cyrus Daly was not the first client to get cold feet at the last minute.

Upon landing, Sokolov rented a car under a false identity and headed to a hotel to prepare. He was carrying a case that contained the makeup, wigs, and other supplies he would need to transform himself.

He had plenty of time to get ready for his performance, as he planned to appear at the cabin in the early morning hours. Blake's bodyguard would be jarred from sleep and on edge. Sokolov would seek to be seen by the man away from Blake, but it didn't matter if Blake was nearby or not.

Sokolov knew from experience that his sudden appearance was enough to make someone drop their guard. More than once he had been seen while dressed in the guise of someone trusted while that person was already present. On those occasions, the confusion seeing double produced left the target's defenders stunned. They died in their bewilderment as Sokolov acted first.

After checking into his room, he unpacked, then went down to the hotel's restaurant for dinner. As he ate, he studied the driving directions to the cabin by using his phone. He couldn't remember lines of dialog to save his life but Sokolov had always been great at memorizing driving directions. When he was sure he had the directions down, he looked at the local weather forecast. It was to be a clear night, but moonlight wouldn't be much of a factor since there was no more than a sliver of the orb in the sky.

After finishing his meal, Sokolov returned to his room and laid down for a nap. He set the alarm to wake him so that he would have ample time to transform himself into Warren Blake.

TARAN LEFT HIS VEHICLE AND HIKED TOWARD THE cabin, making it into the area just before dark. He was carrying a gun on his left hip, had a canteen of water secured to his belt, and a sniper rifle hung across his back.

There was a hill near the cabin that was a natural choice for a sniper. Taran ignored it. Instead, he climbed higher and set up at a greater elevation that afforded him a superior view of the cabin and its surroundings. It also placed him six hundred yards away. Taran was fine with that. He was as deadly at that distance as most men were at thirty feet.

By the time night had fallen, he was settled behind a makeshift shooting blind he'd assembled using branches and dried leaves. The cabin stood out like an oasis thanks to the light on the front porch. The scope on his rifle was capable of night vision if he desired. It was unlikely he would use it because the cabin was beyond the range of the device. The glow of the cabin's porch light was sufficient to illuminate any targets. If an opportunity arose, Taran would be ready.

TANNER WAS ON THE CABIN'S PORCH, SEATED ON THE floor with his back leaning against the wall. There was a low-watt bulb lit in a fixture above the door. Other than the one light, it was dark out.

Across from Tanner was a piece of patio furniture. It blocked his view but also kept him from being seen by anyone who might approach the cabin. If someone did grow near, Tanner knew the dog would alert to their presence and warn him.

They had shut down the propane generator as they did every night. Even positioned away from the cabin and in its sound-dampening shed it produced noise that could mask an attacker's approach. The porch light and the other few electrical needs were being supplied by the energy stored in a set of deep-cycle batteries. It had been clear weather all week and the solar panels had absorbed enough sun to recharge them.

Lucky was lying beside Tanner. He had left the porch only once to pee, then returned to his side. He seemed alert and aware that they were doing more than just enjoying the night air. Twice, he had sniffed the breeze and tensed up, as if he caught the scent of prey. Both times Lucky had relaxed seconds later. Tanner had listened intently and heard nothing.

The scope attached to his rifle had FLIR capabilities, Forward-Looking Infrared, which would allow him to see thermal images. It would detect the heat signature of an attacker and give Tanner an advantage in the dark. Its effective range was six hundred yards. Taran's location was at the outer limits of the FLIR system's abilities. Even if Tanner looked right at him through the scope, he might not detect his thermal signature.

Tanner had heard from Pullo and knew that Joe was holding Cyrus Daly for him. Daly had admitted that there was yet another assassin out to kill Warren. Cyrus said the man was a Russian and that

he had been in Chicago the last time he'd made
contact with him. Tanner hoped that meant the man
wasn't nearby yet. He was confident he could stop
anyone from killing his father-in-law, but each
encounter carried the risk that either he or Warren
could be injured. It would be better to avoid a
confrontation and get Warren to safety. Later on, he
could track down the Russian and kill him. If the
man did show himself before they left in the
morning, Tanner would have another grave to dig.

SOKOLOV NEARED THE CABIN WELL AFTER MIDNIGHT
as he hoped to wake up those inside from a sound
sleep leaving them disoriented and at a
disadvantage. Meanwhile, he had enjoyed a good
meal and a rest.

After circling the cabin from a distance to study
it with binoculars, he set up what would be a wakeup
call for the small structure's occupants. Sokolov then
circled back to the narrow dirt road that led to the
cabin. Its front was lit, the light visible through the
trees. Overhead, a great horned owl hooted, as if in
displeasure of Sokolov's presence.

Since it was night, and the real Warren Blake was
likely asleep, Sokolov needed to dress appropriately.
He paused as he neared the glow of the cabin to

begin undressing. He had been wearing jeans, boots, and a tan corduroy jacket. A man rising from bed would not be fully dressed. When he was down to his underwear, he removed a pair of bedroom slippers from the laptop bag he carried and put them on. Appearing barefoot would have been better but the ground ahead would be abrasive. The slippers would do fine and fit the narrative he was creating. His plan was to arouse the house to wakefulness, which would lure the bodyguard outside. After the guard and Blake were separated, Sokolov would pretend that he was Blake. Seeing his employer out in the open and at risk would cause the man to become more on edge. Once the bodyguard's attention was directed elsewhere, Sokolov would kill him.

LUCKY SPRANG TO HIS FEET AND STARED IN THE direction of the driveway. Tanner grabbed him by his collar with his left hand and gripped his rifle with his right. If someone was approaching, he would let them get closer before taking action. If he were to reveal himself too soon, they might disappear among the trees.

The thermal scope was a huge advantage at night, but it couldn't see infrared images through trees. Far better to confront an attacker when they had fewer places to hide.

A soft growl had begun in Lucky's throat. Something or someone was definitely nearby. Confirmation came an instant later as Tanner heard the faint pinging sound the monitor was making inside the house. That monitor was connected to the motion sensors he had placed around the cabin.

Tanner strained to listen for footfalls or the rustle of fabric, and that's when he heard the sound of a gunshot coming from off in the distance.

SOKOLOV MADE IT TO THE CABIN BY USING THE PORCH light as a guide. If the light had been off, he'd have found himself in near total darkness. As he entered the outer edge of the light, he rushed over to duck behind an old pickup truck. He had left behind in the woods a recording of loud gunshots that would be spaced out over several minutes. The recording was on the opposite side of the cabin, so as to draw attention away from his approach.

When the bodyguard responded, Sokolov would be moments away from fulfilling his contract.

Up on the distant hill, Taran had watched Sokolov emerge from the darkness and duck behind the pickup. As he zoomed in on him with the scope, he could see that the man was wearing only underwear. After making another adjustment he was able to see more details. The man appeared to be middle-aged, but he couldn't make out his features because his back was turned toward him. There was a gun in a holster clipped onto the back of his underwear.

When the first recorded shot went off, Taran swiveled his rifle in that direction. While doing so, he caught the movement on the porch as Tanner rose into a crouch to look around.

Taran was startled to see him and surprised he hadn't spotted Tanner earlier. He'd seen the dog leave the porch but was unaware that anyone else was outside. He should have expected to see Tanner since discovering he was Warren Blake's son-in-law. It was no wonder other assassins had failed; Blake had Tanner as a protector. Tanner swiveled his head and Taran saw his eyes. He knew those intense eyes.

But why would he allow Blake to wander around in the dark? Taran asked himself. While still watching, Taran saw Tanner bring up his rifle to use the thermal scope. When Tanner paused while using it to stare toward him, Taran wondered if he'd been detected.

AFTER HEARING WHAT HE TOOK TO BE A FIRED SHOT, Tanner jumped up to stare in the direction it had come from.

Warren shouted to him from inside after the noise had awakened him, his voice filled with sleep and confusion. "Cody?"

"I'm okay!" Tanner said. "Stay inside and keep low while I find out who fired that shot."

"Be careful!" Warren called.

Tanner raised the rifle and used the thermal scope, looking to where the shot had originated. He saw nothing, then realized that Lucky was growling at something behind him. As he brought the scope around to gaze in that direction, he detected a body heat signature up on a hill. Or so he thought. When he checked again, he saw nothing and assumed it had been an animal moving about.

The sound of another shot came from the same area. Tanner leapt over the porch railing and knelt beside a bush while gazing in the direction of the gunshots. It was an act. Lucky was still growling at something behind him. Tanner wanted whoever was there to believe he had fallen for the decoy shots. As someone practiced in deception, Tanner recognized a setup. He spun suddenly with his gun raised and ready to shoot. When he saw Sokolov walking toward him, he took him to be his father-in-law.

"Warren? What are you doing out here?"

Sokolov pointed at the cabin and spoke in a perfect imitation of Warren's voice. While doing so, he made himself sound scared. It wasn't all an act. He hadn't expected to find Tanner fully dressed and looking alert. A second concern was the gun he'd brought along. It was tucked inside a clip-on holster that he'd attached to the back of his boxer shorts. The weapon's weight was threatening to drag the underwear down around his ankles. Sokolov was forced to use one hand to hold on to the waistband of the boxers.

"Someone was trying to come in through the back door, so I went out a window," Sokolov said, while speaking in Warren's voice.

To Tanner, that meant that there might be more than one attacker. He pointed at the pickup.

"Crawl beneath the truck and stay quiet. Don't come out until I tell you to." He looked down at Lucky. A soft growl was still coming from deep in the dog's throat as he stared at "Warren."

"Hush, Lucky," Tanner said, as he turned his back on Sokolov and used the rifle scope to scan the hill where he'd seen a heat signature. The signature was back, and this time it was steady, and closer to the cabin.

~

Taran moved down the hill, his eyes aided by the night vision of his scope. Something was wrong. He'd been staring in the direction of the shots when the second one sounded off and he'd seen no muzzle flash. It could mean that the fired weapon had a flash suppressor, but even if it had, he should have seen something in such inky blackness as the Maine woods possessed at night.

He paused to disengage the night vision mode on the scope so that he could use it normally while also increasing its magnification. It had been several seconds since he'd last sighted in on the cabin and he wanted to see what Tanner was doing.

Tanner had turned toward Warren Blake and was talking to him. It appeared he was telling the man to hide under the truck as he pointed at it. A moment later, Tanner had turned his back on Blake and was using his own scope to scan the hill where Taran stood. Taran assumed he'd been spotted. He was concerned. Taran recognized the configuration of the rifle Tanner was holding. It was an AR-15. Although he was positioned at the far edge of the weapon's range, it was possible a man like Tanner could use it to kill him with one shot.

Taran was about to drop and take cover when he saw the man he thought was Warren Blake pull the weapon from behind his back. He had pretended to be lowering himself to the ground, as if to hide beneath the truck. When Tanner turned away, he had straightened and reached for his weapon. There was a smile on Blake's face as he took aim at the back of Tanner's head.

TANNER WAS SIGHTING IN ON TARAN, WHO APPEARED to be doing the same to him. As Tanner was about to fire, an image of Warren entered his mind and a tingle ran up his spine. Decades of training had spawned unerring instinct in him. A large part of that training had been mental discipline. In particular, the development of superb attention to detail and an excellent memory. Those two traits were about to save his life.

Tanner dropped low, spun, and fired three shots into Sokolov's chest, catching the assassin by surprise as he was about to fire a round into the back of his head. A hole appeared in the center of Sokolov's forehead, above eyes that had been filled with shock.

That round was not fired by Tanner, but by Taran. Although he knew Tanner had a bead on his position, he had stood his ground to make the shot.

Taran had believed he would be saving Tanner's

life. He was as stunned as Sokolov when Tanner dropped and pivoted. Down below, Tanner was once again aiming at Taran. In response, Taran raised his rifle over his head in a gesture of peace.

LUCKY'S GROWL MORPHED INTO A WHIMPER AND HE squatted, his belly pressed against the ground as Tanner fired at Sokolov, but the hound stayed near him. The bullet that entered Sokolov's head did so a millisecond after Tanner had fired his shots. Whoever was on the hill must have seen Sokolov aiming his gun with the intention to kill Tanner. That person had acted to save his life.

It was possible they believed the man lying on the ground was really Warren Blake. If so, then why would Blake want to kill his own bodyguard? Also, why not allow Blake to do so? Once Tanner was dead, they would no longer have to deal with him and could kill Blake afterwards.

But no, the man up in the hills acted to save Tanner's life by firing one unerring shot and no more. As Tanner used his scope to view the man again, he saw that he was standing with his rifle over his head, and not pointed at him. Tanner copied the gesture, knowing the man didn't need an infrared scope to view his figure, which was illuminated by the porch light.

He lowered the rifle a moment later to peer through the scope again. The other man was making his way down to him. Tanner lowered the rifle and took a position on the other side of the pickup truck. As he passed Sokolov's body, he spoke to him as he looked down at the Russian.

"Nice try, but Warren Blake doesn't have hair on the back of his hands."

Sokolov, who had also possessed the ability to pay attention to details had assumed it wasn't necessary to go to extreme lengths to fool Tanner into believing he was Blake. Among the fine points he'd neglected was the removal of hair from his hands. He had considered doing so at one time but presumed that under duress and given the late hour, such a minor difference would go unnoticed as it often had during other contracts. He had underestimated Tanner, and like so many before him he had paid the price.

"Warren!" Tanner called.

"Yes?" Warren called back to him from inside the cabin.

"Are you all right?"

"I am. But that shooting worried me. Are you injured?"

"I killed another assassin. We also have company."

"Company?"

"Yeah. Stay inside until I find out who he is."

Tanner waited as Taran grew closer. The man was walking toward him after detaching his night vision scope to use as a monocular to navigate the hill in the dark. After he reached the bottom of the first hill, Taran was hidden behind the second hill. If he were up to something that would have been an opportunity for him to circle around and approach in stealth from a different angle.

As time passed and Taran failed to appear, Tanner was wondering if that was what the man was doing. When Taran came into view again he did so while calling out to Tanner, to let him know he was there. He was approaching from the right, where the sounds of the shots had come from. Tanner detached his scope from the rifle and raised it to get a better look at him. Taran was a man-shaped blob of red and orange color in the lens of the thermal scope; however, Tanner could estimate his height and weight. The man walking toward him was in shape and possibly a little shorter than himself. In his right hand was a device. It was Sokolov's audio player.

As Taran grew closer he hit a button on the machine. The sound of another recorded gunshot filled the air. Up close it sounded artificial. A moment later and the recording reached its end. Before it shut off, the sound of electronic static could be heard. As Tanner suspected, the shooting sounds had come from a machine meant to act as a distraction. He had used such tactics himself from time to time.

As Taran finally entered the reach of the porch light, with his rifle slung across his back by a strap, Tanner realized he was Asian.

Taran smiled at him as their eyes met, then greeted Tanner with a bow.

"Hello, Tanner. My name is Taran."

"I've heard of you," Tanner said. "I also think I saw you in New York City recently."

Taran bowed again, but more pronounced. "That was me, yes."

"Have you been following me?"

"I followed Mr. Joseph Pullo hoping that he would lead me to you."

"Why?"

"I wanted to meet you."

"But you didn't that day; you took off."

Taran sighed. "I didn't want you to misunderstand my intentions."

"Do you know the name Maurice Scallato?"

"I had heard of him. I also know it was you who killed him."

"Scallato stalked me too. He wanted to kill me to

prove he was the best assassin in the world. Things didn't end the way he thought they would."

Taran grinned. "That is an understatement. And I do not seek your death."

"That assassination of the Bosnian war criminal, that was you?"

"Yes."

"That was an incredible shot you made. The newspapers say it was over fourteen hundred yards."

"Fourteen hundred and thirty-six," Taran said. There was pride in his tone that he couldn't hide.

Tanner looked over at Sokolov's body. "That was a hell of a shot you hit him with too."

Taran gave a slight bow. "Thank you. He is not Warren Blake, is he?"

"No. He was one of us."

"I thought I was saving your life, but you acted first to save yourself... what gave him away?"

"His hands are different from Warren's. It took me a few moments to realize it," Tanner said, and as he spoke, he became aware that Lucky was staring at Taran while wagging his tail.

"You are Tanner number seven, yes?" Taran asked.

"That's right."

"And your sensei, your predecessor... does he still live?"

"Yes."

Joy alighted in Taran's expression at that news. "I had feared him dead, since you are not much younger than he. I know his sensei had been much older when he trained him."

Tanner cocked his head. "How do you know that?"

"I met Spenser in Japan when I was a boy. He saved my mother and myself from the Yakuza."

"Why are you here, Taran?"

"I was offered the contract on Warren Blake and refused it. I then decided to prevent his murder."

"Why would you do that? You don't know the man."

Taran's expression grew serious. "The contract had no honor. I wanted to stop it."

Tanner nodded his understanding. Several years earlier he had taken similar actions after being offered a contract on a psychiatrist. At his own expense he had traveled to Colorado from Nevada to save the doctor from death. He wouldn't have thought of it as preventing a dishonorable act, but it amounted to the same thing.

He had saved the psychiatrist, Dr. Jessica White, and by doing so had discovered he was related to her husband. Jessica and her husband were not only family but had also become good friends. Had he not interfered; the situation might have ended in tragedy.

Tanner gestured toward the cabin. "Let's go inside. I'll introduce you to Warren."

Taran smiled again and moved toward the cabin. As he passed Lucky, he petted the dog, who licked his hand in return.

Tanner had still been holding his rifle, but he slung it across his back as he headed up the cabin's steps. His instinct had helped him survive Sokolov. Now it was telling him he had nothing to fear from Taran. The two elite assassins entered the cabin. Behind them, lying dead in the dirt, was a member of their profession unfit to inhabit their league.

20

BUSTED

A<small>LTHOUGH IT WAS BARELY THREE A.M.,</small> W<small>ARREN WAS</small> wide awake after hearing gunshots and fearing for his life. Tanner whispered to him to remember to call him Tanner and not Cody in front of Taran.

Warren shook Taran's hand with a hesitant grip, then told Tanner that he would brew a pot of coffee. Taran asked if there was tea and Warren said he would put on the kettle to boil water.

As Warren moved into the cabin's small kitchen, Tanner and Taran settled in the living room. They were seated across from each other at a small table that held a checkerboard.

"Spenser has mentioned his time in Japan. He was much younger then," Tanner said.

"I had never seen a man like him. He defeated seven men and did so with ease. The Yakuza had killed my father because he owed them money. My mother and I had witnessed the murder and they were trying to kill us to keep us silent. Men had caught up to us outside Tokyo, but Spenser stopped them from killing us. I was nine when I met him."

"Who trained you?"

"My sensei was one of the last true ninjas. Since then, I've sought out other teachers."

"I'll call Spenser in the morning. I'm sure he'd like to talk to you."

Taran grinned. "I too would like that very much."

Warren carried over a pot of coffee, three cups, and a tea bag. After laying them down, he went back to get the tea kettle and packets of sugar.

As they sipped their drinks, Tanner filled Warren in on what had transpired outside.

"He really looked like me?"

"You'll see for yourself when it gets light. He nearly fooled me completely."

When Warren excused himself to use the bathroom, Taran took out his phone. "I have something to show you. It was filmed inside Mr. Blake's home. I entered it to find information that would lead me to him."

Tanner stared at Taran, as the implications set in. "You must have learned a lot about Warren... and me."

"It was not my intent to uncover your true name, Tanner."

Tanner sighed. "I believe you. What do you have to show me?"

Taran played the video that one of his devices filmed inside Warren's home. When it was done playing, Tanner looked up from the screen.

"She's attempting to poison Warren. She probably would have gotten away with it. The police would have thought he'd been killed by one of Hall's hitters."

"I believe you're right," Taran said. "I emptied the contents of that bowl into a plastic bag and placed it in the trash. After washing the bowl, I refilled it with fresh sugar."

"I'll have someone retrieve the bag so it can be tested."

"Is Mr. Blake close to the woman?"

"Yes."

"That is unfortunate."

Tanner rose from the table and walked into the kitchen area. Despite the early hour, he used the satellite phone to call the penthouse. He needed to speak to Sara, and it couldn't wait.

The call ended by the time Warren emerged from the bathroom. He was yawning despite the caffeine boost he'd had.

"I'm tired again. I think I'll head back to bed if you two don't mind."

"Yes, get some sleep, Warren. But set your alarm for six. I still want to get out of here early."

"Do you think there's more trouble coming?"

"I don't know."

"Where will we go?"

"We'll be heading to New York City. I'm going to stash you with Joe Pullo while I finish things."

Warren cocked an eyebrow. "You're leaving me with mobsters?"

"You'll be safe. Joe will make sure of that."

Something occurred to Warren and he smiled. "Will I be staying in that strip club he owns?"

Tanner smiled back. "Sorry to disappoint you, but that club doesn't exist anymore."

"Too bad; that could have been interesting." Warren yawned again. "Goodnight, you two."

As Warren climbed a spiral staircase up to the loft, Taran asked Tanner what he meant by "finishing things."

"Pullo has the man who tried to hire you, Cyrus Daly, but Daly was just a tool of Zander Hall. For Warren to be safe, Hall has to die."

"You are going to kill him?"

"I am. I just need to figure out how. The man is in prison and locked away in a cell for twenty-three hours a day."

Taran's eyes lit up. "A challenging situation. They are my favorite."

Tanner got up, walked over to an old rolltop desk in a corner of the room, and grabbed a file. It contained details about the prison Zander Hall was in. He'd compiled it before traveling to the cabin.

"Two heads are better than one. How about helping me figure out a way to kill Hall?"

Taran sent Tanner a seated bow. "It will be my pleasure."

BY DAYBREAK THE TWO ASSASSINS HAD COME UP WITH a plan to kill Zander Hall. The solution appeared once they abandoned the notion of breaking into the prison or breaking Hall out. Both of those options were possible. They would also have needed weeks, if not months of planning and preparation. What they came up with was far simpler and involved less risk.

Taran volunteered to dispose of Sokolov's corpse. He went out at daybreak and came back with the rented vehicle Sokolov had been using. Inside the trunk was a case containing Sokolov's makeup and wigs.

Warren had come outside to view his double's

body. He said it was like looking at himself lying dead on the ground.

Tanner used the satellite phone to call Spenser in Wyoming. Spenser remembered Taran, whose real name was Kota. Taran spoke to Spenser for several minutes, his eyes were bright with joy at hearing the voice of a man whom he had spent his life emulating.

During their conversation the previous night, Taran had told Tanner he'd chosen to use the name Taran because it sounded similar to the name Tanner. It was his way of paying tribute to Spenser.

WARREN WASHED TARAN'S CLOTHES AFTER THE assassin returned from burying Sokolov's body. Taran showered and put on Warren's robe while waiting for his clothes to dry.

Tanner and Warren would be leaving for a nearby town where they could rent a car to drive to the Bangor Airport. The old Ford truck would be left behind at a repair shop for Warren's friend to pick up.

Taran dressed and joined them outside the cabin. He and Tanner shook hands as they said their goodbyes.

"I hope to see you again someday, Taran. Are you staying in America?" Tanner said.

Taran smiled. "For a time, but my home is in Asia."

"Keep an eye on the news. That will let you know if our plan to kill Hall worked."

Taran held up a hand. "There is no need. Even if the plan fails, Hall is dead. You will kill him no matter what."

"That's true," Tanner said.

Taran had arrived in the area driving a Land Rover. He had collected it when he disposed of Sokolov's body. After saying his goodbyes, he drove off. His destination lay west, as he was going to explore the country.

"I like that guy," Warren said. He was behind the wheel of the pickup truck.

Now that they were alone, Tanner decided it was time to give Warren the bad news. Taran had left Tanner the phone that had the video on it. It had been one of several cheap burner phones Taran had.

"There's something I need to show you, Warren. It's going to come as a shock to you."

Warren's face clouded as he looked at Tanner's expression. "Is something wrong?"

"Watch the video and you'll understand."

Warren did so. When it was over, he shook his

head in confusion. "Was that poison she mixed in with the sugar?"

"That's what I think. The contents of the sugar bowl are being analyzed. I called Sara and warned her. She contacted Jake, and he's having a lab run tests."

"Where did this video come from?"

Tanner explained how Taran had tracked them down.

"Thank God he did," Warren said, "or we might have never known. My God, she could have killed others too. What if I'd been sitting down to have coffee with the family? Even worse, someone might have used the sugar to make a treat for Emily or Lucas." Warren's face reddened with anger, even as tears ran down his cheeks. "I can't believe this."

"Sara's handling it. You won't have to see her again, except maybe in court."

Warren wiped away tears and started the truck. "I would have trusted that woman with my life."

"I'm sorry, Warren. I know it must hurt."

"I haven't felt this betrayed since Lily left me."

Warren placed the truck in gear and headed away from the cabin.

In New York City, Sara greeted Nina as the older woman entered the penthouse. Nina sent her a bright smile then complimented Sara on the penthouse's décor.

Mrs. Johnson was nearby, seated on a sofa. She sent Nina a nod of acknowledgement, but not a smile. Jenny had come by earlier to gather Lucas for a play date with his cousin, Emily. Sara had asked Nina over, saying she wanted to talk to her, to get to know her better.

Nina had just taken a seat on the sofa near Mrs. Johnson when the doorbell rang again. It was Jake. He arrived with two homicide detectives and he had news.

"Strychnine?" Sara said.

"The lab confirmed it," Jake said. He walked over to the sofa and stared down at Nina. "Please stand up, Nina."

"Jake? What is this about?"

"I need you to walk over and stand by the two detectives."

Nina gave him a puzzled look but did as he said. Once she was clear of the sofa, Jake addressed Mrs. Johnson.

"We know that you poisoned the sugar bowl.

These detectives are here to place you under arrest for attempted murder."

Mrs. Johnson opened her mouth in shock. As she attempted to act as if she had no idea what Jake was talking about, he held up his phone, showing her the video Taran had made. Mrs. Johnson gasped and shook her head.

"There are no cameras in that house. How did you get that?"

Jake ended the video and spoke to the detectives. "She's yours."

Mrs. Johnson was frisked and cuffed. As they were leading her away, Sara had only one question.

"Why? Mrs. Johnson, why would you attempt to murder my father?"

Mrs. Johnson's features twisted with hate as she stared at Nina. "Because of this foreign bitch. I cared for Warren for years and he never thought of me as a woman, only a servant. I could have changed his mind if this witch hadn't come along and seduced him. I...I... I want a lawyer."

"It won't be Daddy," Sara said, as the police escorted Mrs. Johnson out of the penthouse.

Nina's eyes were huge in her head. "What just happened?"

Jake played the video again, explaining that Mrs. Johnson had mixed poison with the sugar. Nina was aghast as she watched it.

"Warren adores her. Why would she try to kill him?"

"My guess is money," Sara said. "Daddy told me he's included her in his will. Something I'm sure she knew. If she couldn't have him, I suppose she would settle for getting the money he was going to leave to her."

"Mon Dieu," Nina said.

Jake left the apartment and Sara sat on the sofa with Nina.

"I want to apologize to you, Nina. I think I've been a little standoffish towards you."

Nina smirked. "I did get that impression."

"It's just that it always seems odd to see my father with a woman who's not my mother. It shouldn't. I mean it's not as if my mother treated Daddy well."

"Your father and I love each other, Sara."

"I'm aware, and I'm happy for both of you. Please forgive me for being so distant."

"There's no need to apologize. You were never rude."

"Thank you. And I've good news. Daddy is coming back to the area today. I thought we could go to the airport together to greet him and Cody."

"Yes. I miss Warren so much."

"He won't be returning home right away, but soon the risk will be ended, and everything will be normal again."

"Does Warren know about Mrs. Johnson?"

"Yes."

"He must be so hurt. He loved her as a friend."

"So did I," Sara said, "And I trusted her with my baby."

Nina looked over at the empty playpen. "Where is Lucas?"

"He's with Jenny and Emily. I'll be picking him up after we leave the airport."

"When is Warren's flight due?"

"Not for a while; I was hoping we could enjoy an early lunch in the meantime."

"Fantastique, but I will pay."

"All right, but where would you like to eat?"

"There's a lovely place nearby, next to one of my boutiques. Afterwards, I can show you my shop."

Sara smiled. "I'd like that."

"How long was Mrs. Johnson staying here?"

"For several days."

"Can I make a suggestion," Nina asked.

"Of course."

"Throw out all your food and buy fresh groceries."

Sara laughed. "That's an excellent idea."

21

A PICTURE IS WORTH A THOUSAND VOLTS

Z ANDER H ALL TURNED AROUND, PLACED HIS WRISTS behind him, and backed up to the slot in his cell door. A guard reached in, cuffed him, then unlocked his cell.

It was time for Hall to go out into the isolated section of the exercise yard. Once there, he would spend an hour lumbering about like a caged bear and gazing up at the sky or at the flowing water of a nearby river. It was the highlight of his days. The other twenty-three hours were spent inside his six-foot by eight-foot cell.

Hall figured if he had to keep living the way he was that he would be mad within ten years. He had come to believe he no longer had anything to look forward to. Cyrus Daly had quit leaving messages. Maybe he was dead, or he had gone off to begin his new life. Either way, he hadn't left a new message in days.

Hall rolled his shoulders as he felt the spring sun warming them. He cursed himself every day for deciding to stay and stand trial rather than go on the run and hope to stay clear of the law. Even if he had been caught eventually, he would have spent less time behind bars.

Warren Blake. It was Warren Blake's fault he was locked away forever. The lawyer had let him down. Hall swore that whatever it took he would see that man dead someday. If Cyrus couldn't do it, he'd make contact with someone who would.

Hall paused in mid stride as something up in a nearby hill caught his attention. It had looked as if light was reflecting off glass. As he squinted to see what it was, he realized it was growing closer.

The shiny object arrived within moments and hovered over the prison. The noise it made was muted by the sound of an airliner passing overhead. When the object lost altitude and dropped down inside his fenced-in area, Hall stepped back to give it room. It was a drone, a white one, and there was something attached to it.

The two guards watching him had been yammering with each other about a baseball game they'd seen on TV the night before. When they realized what was happening, they told Hall to step away from the small aircraft. Hall was about to do that when he saw what was attached to the drone and began laughing. It was a photo of Warren Blake. The worthless lawyer was lying on his back in the dirt. He had been shot in the head and had three distinct wounds in his chest. There was a caption at the bottom of the photo written in script. Hall recognized it as being Cyrus Daly's handwriting.

Turn the picture over for more good news.

The guards had unlocked the gate and were shouting at Hall to step back. Before they could get to him and drag him away, he had to see what was on the back of the photo. Hall reached down to grab an edge of the picture and came into contact with a wire. It sent enough electricity into him to cause irreparable damage to his heart. Hall fell to his knees with the flesh of his right hand burnt, and his eyes fluttered from the shock he'd received.

The guards reached him as the drone took to the air again. The last thing Hall ever saw was the drone zipping away over the waters of the nearby river. He was dead before the small craft blew apart from the explosives hidden within it.

THREE MILES AWAY ALONG THE RIVER, TANNER dropped the controller he was using into a trash receptacle that was a recycled fifty-five-gallon drum. The device was heavier than the other garbage. It slipped past the food wrappers and empty soda cans to make a clanging noise as it struck bottom.

The drone had been equipped with cameras that allowed him to view Hall and his surroundings. Duke had one of his contacts create the lethal device.

Taran had been the one to suggest using a drone with explosives, but Tanner had refined the plan by altering it to use electric shock. It lessened the risk that the explosion might injure one of the men guarding Hall.

The explosive still came in handy when it was time to dispose of the drone. It was in pieces and drifting toward the bottom of the river.

Now Warren was finally safe and could return to his life. Information gathered from Cyrus Daly would also give comfort to the relatives of the jurors who had gone missing. Under extreme duress, Cyrus had disclosed the locations of the missing jurors' bodies, along with other information and given access to his funds.

Tanner had killed Cyrus before dealing with Hall. His body would never be found.

Tanner called Joe Pullo as he was driving home.

"It's done. Tell Warren he's a free man."

"Will do. I'll have Red give him a lift home."

"Thanks, and thanks for having Finn Kelly guard him."

"Are you kidding, buddy? When it comes to favors, I'm way behind you. Anyway, your father-in-law is all right. And it doesn't hurt me to get in good with a defense attorney, although I hope I never need him."

"Sara and I are still in the city for a few more days. Why don't we meet for breakfast tomorrow at that diner near where you used to live? They still have the best coffee in the city."

"Sounds good, say eight o'clock?"

"Right, see you at breakfast," Tanner said. He was glad to end his role as protector. He was more suited to be an attacker. Then again, one good thing came out of the experience. He turned his head and spoke to his companion. "I'm beginning to think I'm stuck with you, mutt."

Sitting in the passenger seat with his head out the window, Lucky looked as if there was no place he'd rather be.

Tanner smiled. "I guess there's plenty of room for a dog at the ranch."

TANNER RETURNS!

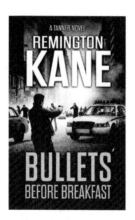

BULLETS BEFORE BREAKFAST - TANNER 31

AFTERWORD

Thank you,

REMINGTON KANE

JOIN MY INNER CIRCLE

You'll receive FREE books, such as,

SLAY BELLS – A TANNER NOVEL – BOOK 0

TAKEN! ALPHABET SERIES – 26 ORIGINAL
TAKEN! TALES

BLUE STEELE - KARMA

Also – Exclusive short stories featuring TANNER,
along with other books.

TO BECOME AN INNER CIRCLE MEMBER,
GO TO:
    http://remingtonkane.com/mailing-list/

MISSING - A Tanner Novel - Book 37

CONTENDER - A Tanner Novel - Book 38

TO SERVE AND PROTECT - A Tanner Novel - Book 39

STALKING HORSE - A Tanner Novel - Book 40

THE EVIL OF TWO LESSERS - A Tanner Novel - Book 41

SINS OF THE FATHER AND MOTHER - A Tanner Novel - Book 42

SOULLESS - A Tanner Novel - Book 43

The Young Guns Series in order

YOUNG GUNS

YOUNG GUNS 2 - SMOKE & MIRRORS

YOUNG GUNS 3 - BEYOND LIMITS

YOUNG GUNS 4 - RYKER'S RAIDERS

YOUNG GUNS 5 - ULTIMATE TRAINING

YOUNG GUNS 6 - CONTRACT TO KILL

YOUNG GUNS 7 - FIRST LOVE

YOUNG GUNS 8 - THE END OF THE BEGINNING

A Tanner Series in order

TANNER: YEAR ONE

TANNER: YEAR TWO

TANNER: YEAR THREE

TANNER: YEAR FOUR

TANNER: YEAR FIVE

The TAKEN! Series in order

TAKEN! - LOVE CONQUERS ALL - Book 1

TAKEN! - SECRETS & LIES - Book 2

TAKEN! - STALKER - Book 3

TAKEN! - BREAKOUT! - Book 4

TAKEN! - THE THIRTY-NINE - Book 5

TAKEN! - KIDNAPPING THE DEVIL - Book 6

TAKEN! - HIT SQUAD - Book 7

TAKEN! - MASQUERADE - Book 8

TAKEN! - SERIOUS BUSINESS - Book 9

TAKEN! - THE COUPLE THAT SLAYS TOGETHER - Book 10

TAKEN! - PUT ASUNDER - Book 11

TAKEN! - LIKE BOND, ONLY BETTER - Book 12

TAKEN! - MEDIEVAL - Book 13

TAKEN! - RISEN! - Book 14

TAKEN! - VACATION - Book 15

TAKEN! - MICHAEL - Book 16

TAKEN! - BEDEVILED - Book 17

TAKEN! - INTENTIONAL ACTS OF VIOLENCE - Book 18

TAKEN! - THE KING OF KILLERS – Book 19

TAKEN! - NO MORE MR. NICE GUY - Book 20 & the Series Finale

The MR. WHITE Series

PAST IMPERFECT - MR. WHITE - Book 1

HUNTED - MR. WHITE - Book 2

The BLUE STEELE Series in order

BLUE STEELE - BOUNTY HUNTER- Book 1

BLUE STEELE - BROKEN- Book 2

BLUE STEELE - VENGEANCE- Book 3

BLUE STEELE - THAT WHICH DOESN'T KILL ME- Book 4

BLUE STEELE - ON THE HUNT- Book 5

BLUE STEELE - PAST SINS - Book 6

BLUE STEELE - DADDY'S GIRL - Book 7 & the Series Finale

The CALIBER DETECTIVE AGENCY Series in order

CALIBER DETECTIVE AGENCY - GENERATIONS- Book 1

DEMONS - A Detective Pierce Novel - Book 2

ANGELS - A Detective Pierce Novel - Book 3

THE OCEAN BEACH ISLAND Series in order

THE MANY AND THE ONE - Book 1

SINS & SECOND CHANES - Book 2

DRY ADULTERY, WET AMBITION -Book 3

OF TONGUE AND PEN - Book 4

ALL GOOD THINGS… - Book 5

LITTLE WHITE SINS - Book 6

THE LIGHT OF DARKNESS - Book 7

STERN ISLAND - Book 8 & the Series Finale

THE REVENGE Series in order

JOHNNY REVENGE - The Revenge Series - Book 1

THE APPOINTMENT KILLER - The Revenge Series - Book 2

AN I FOR AN I - The Revenge Series - Book 3

ALSO

THE EFFECT: Reality is changing!

THE FIX-IT MAN: A Tale of True Love and Revenge

DOUBLE OR NOTHING

Printed in Great Britain
by Amazon